the k-frost caper

james blakley
the
K-Frost
Caper
THE POWERS THAT BE
PUBLISHING

Publisher: The Powers That Be Publishing

Paperback ISBN: 978-1-7362537-2-4
eBook   ISBN: 978-1-7362537-3-1

1 3 5 7 9 10 8 6 4 2

Thanks to God for everything. First, for giving me a wonderful, hard-working family, who raised me, supported me when I was nothing, and encouraged me to achieve my first feat of fiction. For the blessing of tremendously talented teachers, professors, friends, and colleagues who helped broaden my mind. For the flair for fiction and for the guts to go where I've had to in order to make it grow. And finally, for three great states among the fabulous fifty: Missouri (where I learned what I know); Kansas (where I've used it to survive); and Oregon (where Inkwater Press's top-notch editing, production design, and customer service assistance to The Powers That Be Publishing has given me the opportunity to thrive).

in his ears made it hard to hear anything. But Jorge clearly saw a fire truck pull up to put out a burning pillar of orange flames that used to be his home.

CHAPTER ONE

A Big Gamble

It was the only sign of civilization for miles in each direction: A glowing gatehouse sandwiched between two window-speckled towers. Oklahoma's idea of an enchanted castle soared above the leafless limbs of the surrounding winter wilderness. But the warm, yellow glow from the adobe-colored abode wasn't the only thing that drew caravans of travelers. What brought them out was what was inside: *The Moon-glow Casino.* Every night, gamblers (hoping to hit a hot streak) and feverish thrill-seekers (ready to play the slots) poured into the parking lots.

From tonight's sea of seekers a big man surfaced. He wore a heavy, wool-collared coat and his leathery skin stretched over a head of gray hair that was braided into a ponytail. It was all tethered by a bolo tie, making the big man look like a big balloon. He scanned the room, looking past the rows of slot machines and craps tables for something else. He didn't find it; so, after a minute or two, he moved on.

It wasn't long before the big man finally saw something: A set of glass double doors on the far side of the casino floor. He rushed towards them. Once there, he pushed the doors open and entered what was a room on the other side. The big man stopped and looked around. Inside was dim. The only lights came from the table lamps and backlit shelves of booze behind the bar.

The big man didn't see anyone right away. So he found what looked like a quiet table and took a seat. *So much for silence!* A thin waitress, with dark hair that was longer than her skirt, immediately appeared. "What'll it be? A shot or two of something?" she asked.

"Nothing," the big man replied. "I only drink when I am alone."

The waitress turned up her nose and left. So the big man sat, silently killing time by looking blankly at a menu that he didn't plan to order from. Suddenly, a husky "hello" invaded his privacy. Again it was a female voice, but not that of the waitress. When the big man looked up, he saw a much older woman. Her skin was the shade of cinnamon and her raven-colored hair matched her bolero jacket, jeans, and boots. The woman asked if she could sit. Finally, the big man found what he was looking for. "Sit," he told her.

The woman took a seat on the other side of the table and greeted the big man by name. *"Lobo,"* she said.

The man gave a confirming nod. He didn't need to ask who the woman was. "You're Luna Nightcrow," he said.

The woman's lips stretched into a thin smile. *"Bingo,"* she replied.

"Can I buy you a drink?" Lobo asked.

"I'll settle for a clue, instead," Luna replied. Then she leaned over the small table towards the big man. "For instance, Lana says you can help me find something."

"I hope it is love because I would love to snag me some Cherokee..."

"Then get a room...*for yourself, Lobo!*" Luna cut short his romantic hopes. "Besides, Lana doesn't seem like the type of woman who shares her man."

Lobo folded his fat fingers over his belly and laughed, *"Her man?* Lana Ghostwolf keeps my bed warm and my beer cold—*that's all!"*

"Not quite," Luna remarked. "She's tired of that, and wants a new life. So I told Lana that telling me where the talisman is might just get her clear of you; and her record, clean."

"There isn't enough soap in all the Southwest to scrub her past clean! Anyway, Lana could have simply overheard me telling a wild story to some old friends. Now, she thinks she is on to something. Lana will say anything, do anything..."

"Sounds like she learned pretty well from you," Luna interrupted.

"Luna Nightcrow, you are working for the wrong side. You are almost as crafty as me—and could make even more than me, with your looks."

Luna's looks toughened. "We know you have the talisman, Lobo."

"And you think I will roll on the thieves who gave it to me?"

"*Not easily,*" Luna snorted, not lost on Lobo's size or position. "But maybe more money will move you. The company that I represent has the talisman heavily insured. I'm sure they and the Cherokee Nation can increase the amount of the reward from $10,000 to say $20,000 for reliable information on its whereabouts. They might add some more for its return—even more, for the arrest of the thieves." Lobo sat still. "Look, it's only a matter of time before it's found. For once in your life, don't you want to be rich *and* a hero?"

"What good is being rich, if you cannot enjoy it in *this* lifetime?"

Luna got the hint. "The marshals can protect you," she said.

"The same way they can clean Lana's record, huh?" Lobo spat Luna's line back at her.

Luna's reaction was harsh, but true. "You think you're above getting caught and convicted because you're a middleman, Lobo. But no matter how far you've climbed up the crime ladder, you're not at the top," she said. "You're still a small fry. And the guys who *are* at the top expect you to take the fall."

"But at my age, falling into prison for 10 to 15 years might mean that I'll never get back up again."

"Think about it, Lobo: You're a snitch by association. With an informer for a girlfriend, who's going to ever trust you again?" Luna said.

Lobo's life was hard—and getting harder. Luna Nightcrow and the Cherokee Marshal Service had him dead to rights as an accessory in the theft of a 19th century talisman from The Cultural Artifacts Institute. And it was as clear as the cold night that Lobo's lover planned to help the authorities recover it (whether he did or not). The fence's days were numbered, if not already done. For that, he would eventually have to have Lana eliminated. But now, Lana and Luna had the power. Two women forced Lobo to make the hardest choice of his life.

Lobo moved out of the shadows and into the table light. "I'm taking a big gamble," he whispered to Luna.

"It's okay, Lobo, we're in a casino," she replied softly, adding a warm smile that she hoped would hook the crook.

Lobo breathed deeply. Then he came out with it. "Forget the money! I can always get more," he said. "If I tell you where the talisman is, the cops have to deal. They have to get me out of..."

Suddenly, someone shouted, *"LOBO!"* It was the waitress. She disappeared from behind the bar and into the backroom.

Lobo looked over his shoulder and through the glass double doors. Outside, the casino floor was a mass of confusion, with gamblers uprooted from their games. Then, like a bolt from the blue, a wave of Cherokee marshals moved through.

Lobo jumped out of his seat. "You bitch! You set me up!" he shouted at Luna.

"NO, NO...*wait!* I don't know what's going on!" she pleaded.

"I'll bet, *but not here!*" Lobo swept by and out the back, leaving Luna astonished and alone in the lounge. But at least she wasn't alone for long.

A marshal pointed in the direction of the lounge. And within seconds, the entire force burst through the doors with guns drawn. A young man (whose specs and smooth face made him look like a cadet rather than a hard-nosed veteran) ordered the men to spread out. He stopped short of joining them when he noticed Luna Nightcrow still sitting and sulking.

"What's wrong, Ms. Nightcrow?" the commanding officer asked.

"I need a stiff drink, but the waitress is gone," Luna muttered.

"I don't get it—*we got him!*"

"No, lieutenant, we *had* him, until you barged in! You ruined everything!"

"What are you...?"

Before Luna could explain, an unmistakable noise shook her from her seat. Pop-pop—*it was gunfire!* Luna and the lieutenant sprang into action. They raced through the storeroom behind the bar, burst out the backdoor, and into the night air. The lieutenant ran ahead, towards the parking lot, to join his men in the search for Lobo.

Luna was about to follow when a strange sound stopped her. She undid the buttons on her blouse; dipped a hand between her breasts; and unsnapped her Flashbang holster. She wrapped her cold fingers around a warm .38. And with weapon in hand, Luna followed her ears on a search for the source of the sound. Step-by-step through the shadows, the sound grew in clarity and severity. It led Luna back towards the lounge. Then, her eye caught a sudden movement. She whirled sideways. And through gun sights, Luna spotted something propped against the dumpster. *It was a body!*

"Lobo!" Luna gasped.

The big man moaned. Two holes—*bullet holes*—gouged his chest. Lobo was losing blood fast. Luna hurried over and kneeled down. She stowed her gun and removed her bolero jacket. Luna wadded the jacket into a ball and applied it to the wounds, in a desperate attempt to stop the bleeding—to save the man with the talisman.

Lobo gurgled and coughed. He babbled something:

"Two shots...to drink." But when he recognized that it was Luna at his side, the big man tried to focus what little strength he had left. "Luna!" he wheezed. "Looks … true: Casinos make a killing off customers! Too late for me …"

"No! Not yet!" Luna begged Lobo to hang on.

"But not to be...hero," Lobo sputtered. He motioned for Luna to move closer. She leaned her ear to Lobo's lips. His voice faded like air from a punctured tire. Then, Lobo's eyes closed and his body slumped to one side.

Luna stood. All of a sudden, the sound of approaching footsteps swung her around. It was the lieutenant. He looked down at Lobo, then up at Luna, and asked, "Is he dead?"

Luna nodded. Before she could speak, another round of gunfire broke in. Luna and the lieutenant ran into the parking lot. Orange spurts gave away the shooter's position. The other marshals directed their weapons and returned fire. It was the Fourth of July in January, as the night air crackled and popped with explosions.

The lieutenant, with Luna on his heels, ducked behind his cruiser. Another marshal raced in for cover. "Talk to me, Warfield," the lieutenant told him.

"Shooter on the roof!" the marshal responded.

"I can see that!" the lieutenant sneered.

Warfield readied his automatic rifle. He stood, fired, and ducked below. "Sorry about that, lieutenant. Tahlequah Control sent Buzz; should be here any minute," Warfield replied.

"Buzz?" Luna asked.

"An observation drone," the lieutenant told her. Luna looked into the cold night air for signs of Buzz, but almost got blasted. A bullet bounced off the hood of the car. "Keep your head down!" the lieutenant growled.

The rooftop shooter ceased fire. But the marshals remained crouched behind their cars, ready for action. Out of nowhere, a blaze of white light magically appeared in the night sky. Luna couldn't make out the source. But without the chopping, whirling stir of a helicopter, it had to be Buzz the drone. The disembodied beam searched for the shooter, bathing the casino in intense illumination.

More gunfire (this time, in a steady incline) ripped through the sky. The shooter on the roof aimed for the drone, but missed. The search light continued to shine. Suddenly, the shooter stepped into the light. *It was the waitress from the lounge!* She steadied herself on the ledge of the roof, and dived like a swimmer. Only instead of hitting water, her head hit the pavement some 40 feet below.

The lieutenant stood, holstered his gun, and watched his men race to the scene. *"Dammit!"* he cussed.

Luna knew what just happened. "If the shooter didn't take the fall, she might have ended up like the man she shot."

The lieutenant nodded. "No one to blame now, but her," he sighed. Then he turned to Luna for another answer. "Well, where do we go from here?"

Luna opened the door of his cruiser. "How about out of the cold, for starters, Lieutenant Greentree?" she suggested.

"And then?"

Luna smiled and said, "To get the talisman, of course."

CHAPTER TWO

An Old Tune

"Luna Nightcrow does it again. The state and local news sing your praises. Listen to these headlines: INVESTIGATOR RECOVERS RELIC; FREELANCER FINDS ARTIFACT; and, my favorite, WOMAN-FINDS MAN—TALISMAN. Okay, that last title comes from my granddaughter's college newspaper. She is becoming quite the journalist, yes? Well, to the point, congratulations!" Farad Alms told Luna.

Luna seemed numb to the news, but was ecstatic about the espresso Farad made. The insurance investigator took a steamy sip. "Thanks," she said, to the coffee first and Farad's fanfare second.

Luna didn't have a chance to read the news. She led the marshals to the talisman, drove home, and hit the sack. But opportunity rang, and forced her back. Luna rolled out of bed and into a cold shower. Then she changed into a navy blue pantsuit; a pink, scoop neck top; and pumps. All powered-up, she put the pedal-to-the-metal and headed across town to Chase Tower and the headquarters of Charmed Life Mutual.

Luna sat in the lavish office of Farad Alms, CEO of Charmed Life Mutual and, though Indian, a spitting image of Omar Sharif. Farad sat at his cherry wood desk, reading the news from his computer. And behind him, a large, glass window provided Luna with a sweeping view of chilly Oklahoma City at sunrise. Farad was used to the view but, apparently, not to having a celebrity in his midst. He asked Luna, "Why do thieves believe they can steal something so valuable and well-known and then easily dispose of it for cash?"

"These are desperate times," she sighed. "At least these crooks did it by-the-book: They hired a fence to traffic the goods. The problem was that the fence's girlfriend found out and turned fink."

Farad looked confused. *"Fink?"* he asked.

"Sorry: She was willing to exchange information about the talisman for a cleared criminal record," Luna explained. "The fence caught the same bug and wanted protection and relocation, if he turned it over. It looks like the thieves found out and had him killed. Luckily, the fence made something of a deathbed confession to me."

"And that is what led the police to the relic?" Farad asked.

"*Bingo,*" Luna replied.

"Absolutely amazing! I am sorry that you did not get a chance to celebrate. But thank you for taking my call on such short notice." Farad finally turned his attention from the past to the present. "Luna, Charmed Life Mutual is being cheated by a man called Kelvin Frost," he revealed. "Two-and-a-half years ago we paid out $50,000 for a drowning that involved Frost in Mobile, Alabama, though his body was never found. Recently, an application for life insurance was filed by a Kelvin Frost in Miami."

"*Oklahoma?*" Luna asked.

"No, Florida," Farad replied.

"Do you have a separate, unrelated Florida customer named Kelvin Frost?"

"Not officially, but allow me to explain what I mean," Farad replied. "We were notified by one of our elderly Florida customers about a call he received from someone claiming to be with Charmed Life Mutual. The caller said that we had a life insurance policy from Kelvin Frost in Alabama. That was true. But the caller said that the policy also had the man's name in the beneficiary section, and that we needed his Social Security number to release the payments. The man did have a deceased relative named "Kevin Frost" in Alabama. He thought the caller simply mispronounced the name over the phone, and gave the information."

"And there are probably more people with the name Kevin Frost than there are with Kelvin Frost, right?" Luna guessed.

"Good heavens, yes!" Farad confirmed. "Our preliminary research indicates that there are only a handful of Kelvin Frosts in all of North America."

Luna took a sip of espresso, before she summarized the situation. "So, the scammer gets the man's Social security number; probably creates a new Frost in Miami; and submits an application. Looks like a classic case of identity theft, Farad."

"Not just identity theft," Farad cautioned. "We not only want to stop this instance of fraud, but also make certain that the Kelvin Frost we paid on in Alabama is dead. That he did not simply falsify his death and move to Florida."

Luna saw another reason to catch Frost. "If you might also be looking to recover the original $50,000 payout, the contestability period is up, Farad," she added.

"Not necessarily, Luna. It is true that if after two years from the policy's effective date we cannot find any misrepresentations on the application for insurance, we will not rescind a death claim. But, it is clearly stated that Charmed Life Mutual will not pay benefits for an *intentionally* fraudulent death. So a few days ago we sent Hector Luz, our best investigator from Special Investigations Division, to Miami to examine this matter further."

"And...?" Luna asked.

"Nothing," Farad replied.

Luna persisted. "From whom: Kelvin Frost or Luz?"

"Neither," Farad answered. "Hector phoned us that he landed okay. But then, there was nothing more."

"So...?"

"So this means a lot to the company." Farad stood and moved from his desk towards Luna. He stopped and said, "Luna, we are willing to pay you $50,000: $25,000 for Kelvin Frost and $25,000 for information on Hector."

Fifty thousand dollars was about what most experienced insurance company claims adjusters and investigators made...*in a year!* Farad wanted badly to close the case. But Luna continued to play it cool. "So you want me to smoke out the scam and locate Luz, in that order?" she asked.

"Unless we stop this deceitful behavior, it will continue to put our good name in danger. I do not mean to sound callous, but Hector understands that it is business first," was how Farad answered.

"That's good," Luna replied, finishing her espresso. "You can lose more than money, if you let your guard down in the insurance game."

"That is precisely why we called you: Your smartphone never sleeps, Luna. You're one of the best because you keep your eye on the ball."

"Yeah, my life seems to be all about saving everyone else's," Luna sighed. "I'm all yours, day or night. And luckily, your asking price is right."

The comment gave Farad the relaxing laugh that escaped him through the meeting. He turned and retrieved an envelope from on top of his desk. He handed it to Luna. "You have a plane ticket, $2,000 in expenses, and whatever time you need to.., oh." Farad almost forgot. He reached inside his suit coat pocket and pulled out a flash drive. "This contains the background information on the case."

Luna opened her purse and dropped in the envelope and flash drive. She stood and handed Farad her empty coffee cup and saucer. "I'll be in touch," she said.

Farad was a bit uneasy. "Forgive me, Luna, but an old tune comes to mind: *I've Heard That Song Before*."

Luna smiled at the clever reference. "Mine is a new version," she responded. But she understood what Farad *really* meant.

The two shook hands, and Luna left to the sound of "good luck."

CHAPTER THREE

Outside the Box

In her car, Luna double checked the flight status app on her smartphone and confirmed that the clearing conditions kept everything on schedule. She revved up and returned to her loft apartment to pack. The cold loneliness of the place hastened her pace. Luna dreaded the delay that carrying her .38 through airport security would cause. So she left it, and took out what looked like an ordinary smartphone protector instead. However, the case concealed a 650,000-volt Yellow Jacket stun gun. It was enough of a jolt to bring a grown man to his knees (if only for a short time). Luna fitted the case over her mobile device and continued to pack.

Thirty minutes later, the insurance investigator was ready and out the door again—this time, on the road to Will Rogers World Airport. Mid-morning traffic was light; so Luna navigated the slushy city streets and the cleared interstate with ease. She pulled her silver and black Pontiac Solstice into the airport parking lot an hour before her flight. The security checkpoint lines weren't too long. But the usual handful of problem passengers held things up. Luna eventually passed inspection and boarded the Southern Comfort Airways 737 jet. At 1 p.m., she was finally airborne.

Luna reclined in the spacious warmth of first class. She steadied her laptop (an HP EliteBook 850), inserted the flash drive into the USB port, and punched commands into the keyboard. The screen glowed and Luna prepared to open the Kelvin Frost case files. She thought back to her days as a claims adjuster and how a death benefit claim was one of the easiest to handle. After submitting a legal death certificate and a completed claim form, in due time the beneficiary could expect to collect either a lump sum or an annuity payment.

Luna knew that it wasn't unusual for beneficiaries to collect on a life insurance policy that involved a missing person. It was just harder to do, since many insurance companies withheld payments on suspicious death claims until after a thorough investigation. If a body wasn't found, the policyholder was usually declared legally dead. But, the amount of time for a declaration of death varied from state to state.

So it appeared that the circumstances surrounding Kelvin Frost's death weren't originally worth the time and money to investigate. Luna guessed that the claim was accepted because $50,000 was a relatively small amount to worry over (when most life insurance policies easily involved hundreds of thousands, even millions, of dollars). But now, the matter returned and threatened to bite Charmed Life Insurance. It was understandable that Farad Alms wanted to minimize the bite to a nibble, instead of a gaping tear. And while the contestability period was over, there was a good chance of recovering the $50,000 because any good attorney—and Farad had many—could argue in court that this, beyond a reasonable doubt, was a case of intentional fraud.

But to collect, there had to be someone to collect from—preferably, the perpetrator. The first play in the average investigator's life insurance fraud playbook was to zero-in on the beneficiary as the suspect. Luna did just that. She opened Kelvin Frost's policy file and discovered that the beneficiary listed on the first $50,000 payout was a Shandon Sayers of Mobile, Alabama. The information indicated that Sayers worked part-time for the Veteran's Administration (during a brief remission from cancer). Luna scoured the Web and found a few still-posted news stories about Kelvin Frost's drowning. She also found that they gave some background about Sayers's relation to Frost.

Shandon Sayers went to great lengths to get one of Frost's buddies his benefits. Frost contacted Sayers through an online cancer support group and expressed his thanks. The two became fast cyber-friends. And eventually, Frost listed Sayers as the sole beneficiary on his life insurance policy. After a few more months, Sayers and Frost finally decided to meet face-to-face and planned a weekend getaway at Mobile Bay.

Lifeguards verified that a man left Sayers and entered the water. He swam, but didn't come ashore. A routine search for the body was conducted. But after a week, nothing turned up. And with four other recent drownings in the surrounding area (due to rip tide currents) the local authorities seemed satisfied that Kelvin Frost also drowned, and that his body was carried out into the Gulf of Mexico. Sayers collected the death benefit, though she eventually died a year later from cancer.

Without a living beneficiary or policyholder to question, Luna shifted her focus to the recently-filed Kelvin Frost application. The contact number of the so-called Charmed Life customer service agent was registered to a Miami pay phone. When Luna did a GPS maps search of the exact location, the booth was in a run-down section of town. *What a surprise,* she laughed. And the credit monitoring information wasn't much help because the scammer could use a different name, date of birth, or address along with the real Social Security number that was stolen. In this case, "Kelvin Frost" replaced the elderly customer's name.

So, Luna decided to think outside the box. Who among the people connected with the case (that she had solid information on) could pull this off? Besides Farad and her, only one person came to mind: Hector Luz, the man originally sent to investigate the matter. Luna double clicked on Hector Luz's file for more insight.

Like Farad said, Luz looked like a solid fraud investigator. To go with his M.B.A., he had four years of experience in the insurance business. Luz had solved, or been instrumental in solving, several big fraud cases (though most of them were done from the office). And the two that required fieldwork kept him in fairly familiar Southwestern surroundings. But aside from an occasional minor traffic violation or two, there weren't any disfiguring blemishes on his background or in his Charmed Life Mutual evaluations.

But like any business, insurance relies on people (whether selling it or buying it) to make it go. And since no one is perfect, the first thing that could have led Luz astray was the changing practices of some insurers. Luna remembered when she investigated an insurer that got its parent company to redirect a great deal of its reserves to an offshore entity for reasons other than paying their policyholders' claims. While it wasn't strictly illegal, it was definitely misleading because it made the company look like it had millions for claims payouts when the offshore entity was using the funds. It was just one of a growing number of gray areas that allowed room for insider scheming.

Hector Luz looked into a variety of frauds. After awhile, he could easily setup his own scam; cover it up; and dodge the authorities. Also, to look at him, Luz would be the last person most people would consider to be a criminal. When Luna saw the photo of a caramel-colored baby face, she thought that the only gun Luz might use is a staple gun! But such sweetness and innocence *were* weapons: They could be used to instill trust (the most important part of a successful scam).

But what would Luz's motive for committing fraud be? Luna asked herself. Was it for more money? Farad probably paid Luz a pretty penny to stay with Charmed Life. But maybe someone else paid him more to setup a scam for them. Was it the boredom of being behind a desk most of the time? About four years in was when Luna felt it was time to get out, and decided to become an independent fraud investigator. But with that freedom came a lot of pressure, the greatest being the pressure to succeed at almost every turn. Because she was on her own (with no safety net and no one else to blame for failure). Maybe Luz couldn't afford to lose the stability and perks that the 8-5 provided and planned the Frost fraud as a gradual way out.

Without much solid evidence to go on so far,

filing Hector Luz as a suspect at least kept Luna's senses sharp. When it's all said and done, Luz probably tired from the constant calls from the home office for updates and simply turned off his cell and computer for awhile! Luna laughed to herself. That gave her the idea to disconnect the flash drive from her laptop. Luna instead clicked on the Web and simply surfed, until lunch was served.

CHAPTER FOUR

Heating Up

Southern Comfort Flight 213 landed smoothly at Miami International Airport around 6 pm. Luna left the plane and walked to the baggage area. While she waited for her luggage to arrive, her first thought was to call Hector Luz's cell. But, if he was corrupt, Luna's call—even if she tried to hide her number with a star 67 code—might tip him off that Charmed Life increased its search for him. So she didn't call.

When Luna's luggage finally arrived, it wasn't hard to find. *Nor, it appeared, was she.*

A dark-skinned man in a tan cotton suit and black tie spotted her. He folded the newspaper he'd watched Luna from behind and rubbed his goatee thoughtfully. Then he began to move.

Luna gathered her laptop, slung her purse, and extended the handle of her rolling duffel bag. Just as she was about to start up, the man with the goatee slowed her down.

"*Luna Nightcrow?*" the man asked.

"Yes," she answered.

The man introduced himself. "I'm Detective Tiago Toussaint of the City of Miami Police's Criminal Analysis Team," he said, discreetly unfolding his wallet (which displayed a gleaming, gold badge).

Luna produced her ID. It wasn't gleaming, but the smile that accompanied her formal introduction was. "I'm Luna Nightcrow, independent investigator working for Charmed Life Mutual, OKC."

"Nice flight, Ms. Nightcrow?"

"Yes. And it was even better, when I heard it was Miami, Florida I was headed to, instead of Miami, Oklahoma," Luna laughed. "I'm down here on a fraud investigation case."

"I know," Tiago replied. "And I'm here to tell you that things might be heating up."

Luna grinned. "Your 75 degrees cold snap would be a welcomed heat wave back in snowy Oklahoma!"

"I wish I meant the weather, Ms. Nightcrow. But it's about your case," Tiago replied. "I've been asked to take you to Central District Headquarters. Please follow me."

It was dark when the two left the air terminal and arrived at an unmarked, brown car in the parking lot. Luna walked slowly around the back of the car. She noticed a subtle strip of red, white, and blue lights in the rear window and small, mounted antennae. And when the detective opened the passenger side door for her, Luna saw the police radio inside. *It's legit,* she told herself.

Luna stowed her luggage and got in. Tiago climbed in and radioed that he was inbound. Then he started the car; and Luna, the small talk.

"You picked me out of the crowd quick enough, detective," she said.

"You're dressed for success: Suit, heels, and a little bling," Tiago explained. "I don't usually see insurance investigators dressed so well, Ms. Nightcrow."

"Thanks, detective," Luna replied. "More and more, I see police detectives dressing business casual: You know, in polo shirts and Dockers. So, it's nice to see one dressed to the nines."

Tiago grinned and added, "I also noticed that, even though you're a visitor, you didn't fit in with the others—the tourists in Hawaiian shirts, sun dresses, short shorts, and sandals, I mean."

"Well, that's what they say: "When you're in a big city, don't look like a tourist"," Luna remarked.

"I'm afraid it still won't stop you from being robbed, stabbed, or shot."

"Yeah, the chances of death are 100 percent in the end, aren't they?"

Tiago steered the car through airport traffic and finally reached a turnoff that led to the main road out of Miami International. "Been down here before, Ms. Nightcrow?"

"In Florida, yes; but to Miami, no," Luna said. "I was up in the panhandle one summer 3 years ago on a case. But, I did my *Miami for Dimwits* due diligence in flight though. So watch out, detective: I know the sports teams, seasonal temperatures, and time zone for this town."

"It's always good to see someone who's prepared because "this town" can be deceiving at times."

Luna laughed, "Seriously though, all I know is what I've read from travel guides and tourist blogs—*fluff.* But, now that you're here, I can count on the police to provide me the meat-and-potatoes, right?"

"As long as we still get a taste of what you cook up, Ms. Nightcrow," Tiago replied.

Luna got the point. "Right, right: This is *your* turf, detective. And you don't want to be shown up by some Okie out-of-towner."

"No more than you would want to be dissed by some South Florida city slicker, Ms. Nightcrow."

Luna smiled and said, "Well, now that we have the rules down, detective..."

"Game on, Ms. Nightcrow," Tiago said.

CHAPTER FIVE

Frost in Miami

Tiago pulled into the basement garage of Central District Police Headquarters and parked. He led Luna to the front desk, where she signed-in and was issued a visitor's badge. Luna clipped it to the lapel of her jacket. Tiago found the elevator, and the two rode up to the office of Captain Mikhailah Alexander.

As the leader of the Criminal Analysis Team, Alexander had a big office. But, the only real luxuries in it were a comfortable leather chair and a reliable computer. She dressed the pantsuit part of someone who would populate such a place, but maintained a street cop's no b.s. toughness. And, despite having 4 children, she still had lean, dark brown beauty queen looks (which was more of a luxury for *Mr. Alexander*). Looks aside, Captain Alexander was all about balance and perspective. And in a department whose job was not to just catch criminals in shoot'em-up style, but more often to ensure their successful prosecution by careful collection and analysis of evidence, a level head and keen insight were essential.

Tiago officially introduced Luna to his superior. After shaking hands, Captain Alexander returned to the leather chair behind her desk. Luna took a seat beside Tiago, and the trio began to dig into the case.

"Part of my job is to contact Hector Luz, an insurance investigator with Charmed Life," Luna said.

Alexander nodded. "Charmed Life's been looking for him since late Tuesday," she confirmed. "We told them to give it more time, before filing an official police report. It's only been a little less than 24 hours since they called."

"And hoping to find someone right off the bat like that is a tough job. This is a *big* city," Tiago added.

"But this is potentially a *big* case," Luna gently reminded the detective.

"Definitely," Alexander agreed. "That's why we advised them to wait at least one day. They received a cell phone call from Luz at the airport that said he arrived. So the circumstances surrounding his failure to report might be that he is in contact with a confidential source or is working undercover. Charmed Life said they would send another investigator. Now that you're here, Ms. Nightcrow, we hope you can pick-up the slack.

"This will sound like an excuse, but department manpower is stretched thin. With a key economic conference between The Commerce Department and several Latin American nations underway, we've had to prioritize. For example, airport pickup is usually a two-person detail, with one uniformed officer and a detective. But we sent one detective, though he's one of our best. So again: Any help we can get from an investigator of your caliber, Ms. Nightcrow, is appreciated."

"Thank you, captain. I'll do my best," Luna replied. "Now, about the other reason I'm here. Charmed Life paid a death benefit on a Kelvin Frost in Mobile, Alabama over 2 years ago, though a body wasn't found. Recently, there was an application for life insurance submitted from a Kelvin Frost in Miami. But Charmed Life hasn't any Florida customers with that name. They suspect fraud from the Alabama Frost, using information from a stolen Social Security number."

"Yes, and that's why we called you in," Alexander replied. "A few nights ago, there was a townhouse fire caused by an explosion—a gas leak apparently. Not unusual, until we found that the residence belonged to a Kelvin Frost."

"Is Kelvin a popular name down here?" Luna asked.

"Not when paired with Frost, it isn't," the captain replied. "Frost died. But the autopsy on the remains showed that he was killed by blunt-force trauma *before* the fire. The perp probably thought that blowing up the place would make it look like

Frost died from the blast, smoke, or burns. Though he was burned beyond recognition, no smoke was in his lungs. What probably happened was that the perp hit Frost over the head, turned on the gas, and *then* tossed a match."

Luna turned to Tiago. "Did you find any evidence at the crime scene: Photos, id, a computer..?" she asked.

The detective shook his head. "None, I'm sorry to say. Is there anything solid from your company's side?"

"Not much. The beneficiary and the policy-holder were online friends who only met face-to-face once—and briefly, at that. The original application for insurance described Frost as a 45-year old white male of slight build, with dark hair, and with no pre-existing conditions. The internet news reports of Frost simply went with the beneficiary's description: That he was "tall, tanned, fit, and in his late 30's." See the inconsistency?"

"One of many, I'm sure," Alexander replied. "The new application, based on stolen information, is a valid case. But, in the Alabama case, people misrepresenting themselves online and on applications happens all the time. Is it done with criminal intent, or just a misguided makeover? Maybe Frost *appeared to be* 30-something to the beneficiary. "Tall" and "slight" are also in the eye of the beholder. And maybe Frost hit the gym and tanning salon *after* the Alabama policy was issued. Those by themselves aren't necessarily enough to argue for fraud—especially at this late stage, Ms. Nightcrow."

"So true," Luna sighed. But, she soldiered on. "Well, what about Frost's neighbors: Any witnesses or suspects?"

Tiago offered someone. "A Mr. Jorge De Martine lived below him," he said. "De Martine's a petty ex-con who got out recently, after serving time for driving the getaway car in a robbery. He was just coming home when the place blew up. He doesn't have any life, health, or renter's insurance or any family that we know of."

"Did he tell you anything about Frost?" Luna asked.

"De Martine, like most of the other tenants in the neighborhood, didn't remember seeing Frost. All he said was that the lights were on sometimes; so he assumed somebody lived upstairs. But very few people personally saw Frost."

"It's likely that more people *did* see him," Alexander said. "But with the times we live in, and now the explosion, they're probably afraid to get involved."

Luna thought she picked up on something. "Detective, you said "most of" and "very few" tenants. So there was *someone* who saw Frost, right?"

"Officially, it was just the land lady," Tiago revealed. "And that was only on the day she rented him the place. But her description is...well, pretty vague."

"*How do you mean?*" Luna asked anxiously.

"The land lady could only describe him as "Hispanic-looking." She's a 72 year-old retiree from North Dakota. Not many Hispanics up there, I'm guessing. But down here, over half of Miami's population is Hispanic. Most of them, though, prefer the term "Latino." Latino refers more to Latin America; and Hispanic, to Spain. And to make matters more confusing, we have light, medium, and dark-skinned Latinos from all over."

And I thought that keeping all the different Native American tribes straight was hard! Luna laughed to herself.

"The rental application from Ms. Crossley didn't have any prior addresses or references for Frost. But, that's not unusual here: Owners will often lease to illegals or to those who will pay cash upfront for several months of rent," Tiago added.

"That seems to be a growing trend everywhere," Luna observed. "Besides, detective, if Frost faked his death in Alabama and stole the Social Security number here, any past addresses or references on a rental application would probably be bogus, too."

"So, Ms. Nightcrow, we're back to square one: No reliable descriptions of Frost," Alexander said.

Luna sighed, "Typical, I guess. After all, when's the last time anyone's seen Frost...*in Miami?*"

Tiago chuckled heartily and even Alexander smiled lightly at Luna's levity. "Well, they don't call it Miami "The Magic City" for nothing: Almost anything's possible," the detective replied. "We questioned a couple of other people. And according to them, it turns out that there *was* another Kelvin Frost in Miami...sort of."

That piqued Luna's curiosity. "Please go on, detective," she said.

"I said "sort of" because *this* Frost was originally a fictitious character that was made up by some New Agers back in the 90's. One of them, Bekka Noon, came to us when she saw that the name of the fire fatality was the same as the character. We thought it was just a coincidence. But when the death became a homicide and when your insurance company called about an investigator who's looking into suspicious activity involving a Kelvin Frost, it looked like there was more going on than met the eye."

"Well, it looks like I have a tougher case than I thought," Luna said.

"Yes, Ms. Nightcrow," Alexander agreed. "You have 3 Kelvin Frosts to deal with. There's the original Alabama policyholder, assuming he's alive; the dead man here; and whoever created the Miami applicant."

"Plus you have to find your insurance investigator," Tiago added.

"Captain, do you mind if I talk with some of the people you questioned again?" Luna asked.

Alexander nodded, but said, "Just remember, Ms. Nightcrow: We understand that your company wants to stop this Kelvin Frost and probably recoup some of the original payout. But, as far as the police department is concerned, the people you plan to talk to are not officially suspects. They may or may not talk to you. Or if they do, it could be with an attorney present."

"I understand, captain."

Alexander stood, which meant the briefing was over. "Detective Toussaint is your official liaison, should you have any further questions or needs while you're here, Mr. Nightcrow," the captain said.

Tiago added, "About Bekka Noon, Ms. Nightcrow: She runs a New Age museum that specializes in ancient antiques and exhibits on ghosts, monsters, UFOs—*Twilight Zone* kind of stuff. It's Downtown, where many of the museums are. I'll give you the address. As for Jorge De Martine, Frost's downstairs neighbor, he's out of a place to live, due to the fire. After questioning, he left. We don't know where he is now."

"Thank you, both," Luna said warmly.

Tiago opened the door for Luna. She walked through and into the hallway. Tiago joined her a minute later.

"Oh, as part of my go-between duty, I should ask if you have a place to stay, Ms. Nightcrow," the detective said.

"You can call me Luna, detective."

"And you can call me Tiago. Of course, when we're officially working..."

"Right, right: Back to detective and Ms. Night-crow. I know."

"So again, Ms. Nightcrow: Do you have a place to stay?"

"No. But I have plenty of expenses; and I'm sure your chamber of commerce would love for me to spend a portion of them on a hotel," Luna said. "But I will gladly accept your advice on which hotel is best for the price."

CHAPTER SIX

Ready to Roll

"We're only sleeping here, not living here," was what Luna's father would say when she was a kid, and the family stayed at hopelessly cheap motels during vacations. But she took the advice to heart and understood why he said it. Luna could keep a good chunk of her expenses for other things that might come in handy, if the case lasted as long as she thought it would.

Tiago recommended a decent, economical hotel called The Palm Paradise Suites. It was only 15 minutes from Miami's Downtown District. But Tiago warned that Miami traffic could easily turn 15 minutes into a half hour ride (unless travelled late at night or early in the morning). The detective drove Luna to the pink, five-story structure that actually featured a few palm trees on the property. Tiago made sure Luna checked-in and entered her second floor suite safely.

He returned to his car, and Luna watched him drive off. She closed the curtains and unpacked.

After Luna fired off an e-mail from her laptop that confirmed her safe arrival to Farad Alms, it was only 8 pm. But she hadn't slept since before finding the talisman back in Oklahoma. So she skipped dinner and went to bed.

Luna's smartphone alarm woke her at 9 am, instead of 7 am. Thirteen hours of sleep was her way of celebrating the successful close of the talisman case. Luna checked the local weather (which, for her, was still hard to believe): Partly cloudy and 60 to start, with an increase in sun, and a high of 75 by afternoon.

Luna showered and then dressed in business attire: A gray skirt suit, a pink shell, and patent leather heels. She collected her laptop, locked up, and visited the hotel restaurant for the complimentary breakfast of biscuits-and-gravy and coffee. Afterwards, she took a cab to the local Enterprise Rent-A-Car and scored a Ford Focus ST with all the options. Of all the goodies, Luna was most grateful for the GPS navigation system.

At last, the insurance investigator was ready to roll. She punched in the route to Bekka Noon's Museum of Modern Metaphysics and was on the road again at about 12:30 pm. Luna pulled up to the museum almost a half hour later. But the closest parking slots were taken; so she found a spot a block away and parked. The 5 minute walk will be nice exercise, Luna told herself. She set out on foot, and finally arrived at the museum at 1 pm.

After paying the $10.00 entrance fee, Luna went inside. She passed through the gift shop to the spacious display floors. Luna quietly browsed the exotic collection of surreal statuettes, bizarre busts, and peculiar paintings while she waited for Bekka Noon to fulfill the needs of her other visitors. About ten minutes passed before a pale-skinned, rail-thin redhead in a green tie-dyed dress greeted Luna. "Hi, I'm Bekka Noon, Curator," she said, in a drawl that belonged north of the Florida Stateline.

Luna proffered a palm. "I'm Luna Nightcrow."

The women shook hands, and Bekka remarked, "Wow, I love the name! It's really yours—like, you didn't make it up?"

Luna smiled. "It's really mine," she assured Bekka. "And I guess that Bekka is short for *Rebecca*, right?"

"No, Bekka's Bekka, I'm afraid. Are you Native American, Luna?"

"Yes, Cherokee," Luna replied. "You don't get many around, I guess?"

"Cherokees, no; but, I do have some Seminole memorabilia if..."

Luna declined; she wanted to get to business. "Thanks, Bekka, I'll have a look at it later," she said. "Do you have a few minutes? I have something important that I would like to discuss with you."

"Sure. I don't have any big tour groups scheduled for today."

"Good."

Bekka walked over to a slim blonde in a pink blouse and light gray skirt. "Sharkie, will you take over for me?" Bekka asked.

"Sure thing," the blonde replied happily.

"Oh, I'm so sorry for not introducing you. This is Sharkie Sayles, my assistant."

Sharkie flashed a winning smile and extended her hand. "It's a pleasure to meet you, Ms..?"

"...Nightcrow. But you can call me Luna."

The women shook hands. "Thanks, Luna," Sharkie replied.

Bekka told Sharkie, "We were talking about our unique names. Why don't you tell Luna how you got yours?"

"I'm big into water sports: Boating, snorkeling—the whole deal. Anyway, my mother named me Sharkie because of the swimming sensation and the kicking she felt in her womb."

"Interesting," Luna said, trying not to laugh.

"Yes, I think so. Well, I have to get going," Sharkie said. "Again, it's a pleasure to meet you, Luna."

With that, Luna followed Bekka to her office. Bekka opened the door, and Luna took a seat. The office looked more like a storage closet, cluttered with old books, maps, and a few knickknacks. It reminded Luna of her history professor's office back in college.

"I'm here to find out some more about Kelvin Frost," Luna began.

Bekka's eyes narrowed. *"Are you a cop?"* she asked with reservation.

Luna took out her ID and handed it to Bekka. She smiled apologetically and said, "I'm sorry for not fully introducing myself, Bekka. I'm an insurance investigator; so you can relax."

"Wow! Do you carry a gun, too?"

Luna took back her ID and laughed, "Not usually: It's a hassle. Like when I came in, I noticed your "no weapons allowed" sign. So I would have to leave my gun in the car."

"Yes. I can see why patrons think they need a gun: Because of our exhibits of monsters, aliens, and all that. But these creatures are probably not evil, just misunderstood."

"What we don't understand, we fear..," Luna replied, borrowing the observation from one of her childhood heroes, Chief Dan George.

"Exactly! I'm so glad you understand, Luna."

"Well, Bekka, I'm interested in why you and your friends created a character called Kelvin Frost in the first place."

"We made him up as the idea for a novel back in the 90's. He was the usual strapping hunk of a man we all dream of: Tall, dark, and, I think they call it these days, *cut*."

"I think you mean *ripped*," Luna kindly suggested.

"I'm sorry. Anyway, I thought-up the name. I wanted it to be cool and unique; so I combined the temperature reading Kelvin and frost. *Get it?*"

Luna smiled weakly and nodded.

"We had all kinds of ideas for him: As an action, sports, or romantic hero. But, all the big publishers we submitted Kelvin Frost story ideas to turned us down. And so did the small presses," Bekka continued. "It was only a couple of years ago when I thought we could use the idea for an e-book. You know, e-books are the big thing now. Anybody can be their own writer and mass-produce books online. It's the latest thing, Luna: A way to show the big-time publishers that they're not all that."

"So did you or your friends ever get the story written and self-published on the Web?" Luna asked.

"No. Everyone got on with their lives, and the idea stayed just that: Another dream drifting through the entertainment ether. Anyway, I talked to one of my other friends who made-up Kelvin with me. She's a blogger who used to be into computers. If anybody could make Kelvin into a successful e-book, it's her."

"And she is...?"

"Quinn Wu," Bekka told Luna: "She teaches at The South Shore School of Modern Studies."

"It sounded like there were more than just you two who created Kelvin. Were there?"

"There was one other guy, but he died in a traffic accident 5 years ago. If Kelvin Frost becomes big, I plan to put Mike in the dedication section of the book."

There was a knock on the door. Bekka excused herself to answer it. It was Sharkie Sayles. She whispered something from outside. Bekka nodded and came back in. "I'm so sorry, Luna, but I have an important delivery that just arrived. I don't know what I would do without Sharkie! Would you like to wait until...?"

Luna stood. "No, I understand, Bekka," she said. "I'll stop back by at another time to ask you a few more questions. Thanks for taking the time you did."

Luna stopped by the restroom. When she came out, she saw a delivery man wheeling an ugly, three-headed gargoyle-looking statue toward the display floors, with an excited Bekka frolicking along.

Luna simply laughed to herself and left.

CHAPTER SEVEN

A Measurable Change

When she returned to her car, Luna looked up the address for The South Shore School of Modern Studies on the GPS. The quickest way was across the bay. So Luna headed out of Downtown and for the causeway. She paid the toll and traveled the length of the busy bridge to the elegant Venetian Islands and then into sunny South Beach.

Luna finally arrived at The South Shore School of Modern Studies at 2:30 pm. School was still in session; so finding a close parking space was hard. Luna found a spot, but had to walk a ways. And all the way, she cursed herself for wearing heels. Though Luna caught the quick looks and outright ogles of more than a few students—male, mostly— that seemed to like her foot fashion choice, *as well as the rest of her.*

The campus architecture and layout were Spanish village-styled, with a soaring clock tower as the central landmark. Below the tower was the administrative office building—Luna's destination. But once there, she was told that Quinn Wu's office was in the Information Technology Building. For Luna, that meant more torture on the tootsies (as she started another trek).

It was closing in on three o'clock, as Luna maneuvered through the streams of students coming out of the IT Building. She saw a Chinese woman, who looked older than most of the crowd, and assumed that it might be the person she sought. It was either a lucky guess or a sign of Luna's deductive prowess; but either way, it was Quinn Wu. Wu agreed to talk. But being in a classroom all day, she wanted some fresh air. So, the two women went to the palm tree-shaded courtyard.

Quinn Wu, 52, was of medium height and slight build. Her glasses and graying hair provided the scholarly air that is necessary to convince students and administrators of a professor's worth. Wu taught a popular elective class on creative blogging and e-book design. "That's right: E-books *are* the big thing nowadays," she answered Luna's question about e-book popularity. "I design web pages and do blog tours. I even format e-books. It's a growing online cottage industry, Luna."

"So why not run with this Kelvin Frost idea as

a book?" the insurance investigator asked. "Bekka seemed pretty high on it."

"Bekka's *high* on a lot of things, in case you hadn't noticed," Quinn laughed.

"Like weed, maybe?"

"She used to be. Now, instead of flying high herself, she's into other things that fly through the sky: Angels, ghosts, aliens—otherworldly worries," Quinn responded. "As for why I didn't "run with the Kelvin Frost idea," e-books are popular, but the Big 5 publishing companies still have clout. Everybody dreams about six figure contracts and huge bookstore sales. Not so easy to get, when you self-publish. A lot of do-it-yourself efforts come-off looking amateurish, compared to what most readers are used to picking up in a bookstore.

"So yeah, Luna: Everybody can write his or her own book. But the e-book market's becoming overcrowded. It's hard to get noticed, without a professionally-designed book and marketing approach."

"Bekka says you used to be a computer programmer," Luna said.

"I still am," Quinn laughed. "You don't lose the degree and the title, just because you don't currently use it. Right now, I teach e-book design. But it doesn't take the second coming of Steve Jobbs to do it."

"No, I guess not," Luna replied. Then she changed topics. "I was wondering, Quinn: Why didn't you go to the police when you heard that the person killed in Monday's fire was named Kelvin Frost?"

"Miami is a big place. There are probably *many* people with that name."

"Believe it or not, there aren't," Luna replied.

"Well, Bekka called me and said she was worried. So she went to the police. Then, they came to me. But like I told them and you, Bekka's still a little out there."

"Maybe not in this case," Luna said. "The insurance company that I represent recently received an application for life insurance from someone named Kelvin Frost here in Miami. But their records didn't show anyone down here with that name. Officially, there was a policyholder named Kelvin Frost in Alabama. A little over two years ago, he drowned. And the policy paid $50,000, although a body was never found. But when a Kelvin Frost died here in a fire, there's the possibility that *he* was actually the one from Alabama. That he faked his death before, but died recently."

"And *our Kelvin* fits in how?" Quinn asked.

"The new application that was filed was done with information stolen from a Social Security number. And your character fits a real-life description of the beneficiary in the original Alabama case. Your Kelvin Frost could be the inspiration for a case of identity theft and insurance fraud, perpetrated by either the Alabama Frost or someone who knew about the character."

There was a slight change in Quinn Wu's hospitable manner. "How terrible," she said, though Luna didn't feel any sincerity in the expression of shock. The professor looked at her watch. "Luna, please don't think I'm rude for cutting you short, but I have another class in 10 minutes. Do you have an office where I can stop by or a number where I can call?" she asked.

"I have a number, but not an office. I'm staying at a hotel," Luna answered. She took a pen and a piece of paper from her purse, wrote down her contact information, and handed it to Quinn. "It was a pleasure talking to you. I learned a lot about e-books and blogging," Luna said.

Quinn looked at the contact information. "I learned a lot of things, too," she replied.

"Well, good-bye, Quinn. Maybe I'll hear from you again," Luna said.

"Oh, who knows? But if you decide to write your own book, look me up. I can set you up with a great online promotional package."

Luna nodded and left.

Obviously Quinn Wu (and any normal person) wouldn't think of calling the cops about the death of a man whose name coincidentally belonged to a fictional character created over 20 years ago. But the question got the response Luna hoped for: A measurable change in the professor's manner. Quinn also said she had another class. But Luna remembered something from her past college days: That there weren't very many classes scheduled for 3 p.m. because professors needed time to prepare for or relax before evening classes at 5 pm. With that in mind, she decided to revisit the administrative building.

Once there, Luna found a kiosk outside the Registrar's Office. She picked through the various brochures and fliers and found what she was looking for: A course catalog. Back in the day, course catalogs contained (among other things) class schedules. It was no different now; and Luna looked up Quinn Wu's. She discovered that her next class *wasn't* at 3 pm. That didn't mean that Quinn didn't have a tutoring session, conference, or other *class-related* activity. But, as an attorney might observe, such a contradiction could call her credibility into question. In the end, it looked like Quinn gave Luna the slip. But for what reason, she didn't know.

Luna decided not to make a big deal of it. She only had a few leads and didn't want to scare or anger one over a seemingly small inconsistency. So the insurance investigator played it cool and left. Her feet couldn't have been happier because walking all over campus in heels was grounds for cruel and unusual punishment, murder—almost any number of crimes and punishments!

CHAPTER EIGHT

A Thrilling Tail

Luna dialed-up Central District Headquarters on her smartphone. She asked for, and received, permission to checkout the Kelvin Frost crime scene on her own. As part of the investigation, technically, she didn't need permission. But, it was a tactic taken from any good insurance investigator's playbook: Recognize and suck up to local authority to make them less afraid and more likely to cooperate.

Luna drove back to The Palm Paradise Suites and changed into more suitable crime scene investigation attire: That consisted of a plain T-shirt, jeans, a windbreaker, and tennis shoes. As Luna pulled out of her hotel parking spot, another car started up. The white subcompact waited for Luna's Ford Focus to enter traffic before it did the same.

Two blocks whizzed by without Luna noticing much (except for the plentiful palm trees). She just happened to look off at one when, in her driver's side mirror, she spotted the small white car that she'd thought nothing of a few minutes ago. Luna shrugged. Still nothing to text home about, she told herself.

The drive remained beautiful, but uneventful. Mostly red, black, and blue vehicles, with an occasional loud-colored car, motored alongside Luna. Just a normal flow of traffic along the scenic stretch of Palmway Freeway—that is, until another check of the rearview mirror. A familiar white car turned up. And this time, it didn't take Luna long to realize that she *was* being followed, and in a fairly professional manner. It wasn't an amateur bumper-to-bumper tail, but a steady, carefully-concealed pursuit.

Luna decided to shake things up. She changed lanes and then hit the gas. That spooked the driver of the white car—just what Luna hoped for. The white car slid into the same lane as Luna. But this time, it didn't have another car shielding it. Luna should have had a perfect view. But since she sped up, she was too far ahead to see the license plate clearly. And the driver of the white car suddenly lowered the sun blinder; so Luna couldn't see a face either.

A truck signaled and slipped in between Luna and the white car. *This was her big chance to escape!* Luna could easily outrun her chaser with another quick pedal-to-the-metal burst. Suddenly it occurred to her to let the car continue to follow. That way, I can speed up, slow down, and play around, until the driver slips up and shows a license plate or face, Luna thought.

Luna got out her smartphone and hit what she thought was the speed dial. But when Frank Sinatra answered with a smooth serenade, she realized she hit the wrong button. The diversion caused her to slow down. All of a sudden, there was a...*HONK!* Luna saw the truck driver behind her raring to go. She turned the wheel toward the slow lane, but almost too soon! Another angry beep came from the car next to her.

Luna stopped fiddling with her phone and flipped it aside. "Sorry, Francis, but if I don't tune out, *I'll Be Seeing You* could mean in eternity!" she said.

She finally steered into the slow lane and looked through the rearview mirror again. The white car took a sharp turn and disappeared down the slope of an off ramp. *"Damn!"* Luna shouted.

When she calmed down, Luna picked up the smartphone and successfully hit the speed dial. "City of Miami Police..," the voice on the other end of the line began to say.

Ten minutes later, Luna arrived at the Riviera Row crime scene without a problem (and without company). The string of townhouse apartments was still a rainbow of colors, except for one burned-out black building. *The story of my life,* Luna laughed to herself. Such beauty and happiness all around, but I choose the dark side of things!

Luna locked her smartphone and laptop in the trunk and entered Jorge De Martine and Kelvin Frost's building. For about 10 minutes, she explored De Martine's old digs. There wasn't much left: Mostly scorched wood and ashes. So Luna exited and found the stairwell leading up to Frost's apartment. The stairs looked relatively intact. But Luna stepped carefully and quietly, feeling for any holes or loose boards that might cause her to fall. Slowly and steadily she climbed; until finally, she safely cleared the stairwell and entered Frost's apartment.

This time, Luna took a bit more care when searching. Patches of blue sky shone through holes in roof. It provided enough daylight for her to look up, down, and around the rubble for missed clues. But Luna began to see that the cops probably found everything important here too. So what exactly was she looking for?

Perhaps it was trouble.

A loud *crunch* startled Luna. Was it just the wind? Did a bird fly in? Or maybe the thrilling tail wasn't over: The white car might have tracked her down. That sound could be the driver looking around...*for me!* Luna worried silently. When the shock subsided, she slipped into a shadowy section of the apartment for cover. The crunch became crunches—*footsteps!* Luna automatically reached for her smartphone, but realized it was in the car. *Damn!* She felt around in the dark for something to use as a weapon. Her fingers finally found it: A wooden board. Luna grasped it and slowly raised it to her chest. In the ruins of the room ahead, she sensed someone's presence. Luna decided to see who it was, and rose from her hiding spot.

The last hole in the roof was behind Luna. The rest of the roof was relatively intact, with sunlight only seeping through in places. Now she would no longer have full daylight by which to see. But nor would the other person. The advantage belonged to the one who struck first. So, Luna raised the piece of planking from her chest to her shoulder (ready to swing it like a baseball bat).

Finally, she quietly stepped into the dim room. The intruder, a fat man, was only a few feet away. He was pre-occupied with a piece of debris. So much so that he didn't seem to notice Luna. She closed in like a cat. But at the last minute, Luna stepped on a loose floorboard. The loud *crack* gave her away, and the fat man spun around.

CHAPTER NINE

Knowing an Enemy

The debris fell and the fat man's hands went up in the air, as if to surrender. *"JESUS!"* he gasped.

"No, but you're going to need him, if you don't tell me who you are!" Luna warned.

The crunch of more footsteps distracted Luna. *The fat man had friends!* Luna readied her board for battle. A beam of white light stabbed through the room. But Luna finally dropped her defenses when the owner of the flashlight entered.

"Detective Toussaint! Oh, thank you!" the fat man gushed with gratitude. "You were about to have another homicide on your hands!"

Tiago looked in Luna's direction and grinned. "I don't think so," he replied.

The trio moved back into the daylight. And Luna

removed her ID and showed it to the fat man. "I'm Luna Nightcrow, independent insurance investigator."

In good faith, the fat man removed his wallet from his powder-blue, three-piece suit and nervously handed it to Luna. She looked over his California driver's license. "I'm Umber S. Burroughs," the fat man proudly announced. "You've probably heard of me from *Under the Radar with Umber S. Burroughs?* I'm..."

"*...the celebrity talk-show psychic!*" Luna moaned.

"I prefer the term "clairvoyant," myself," Burroughs replied, retrieving his wallet. "And what's with the hate I sense in your voice? I look into all kinds of legit things: Missing persons, murders—I try to keep it real."

"*And unreal,*" Luna snorted. "What about the conspiracies, aliens, and monsters you also "look into"?"

"Perhaps a demonstration of my harmonious blend of extra sensory insight *and* real world awareness will convince you, Ms. Nightcrow?" Burroughs closed his eyes and reached for something unseen. He seemed to find it—*in Luna*. Then he lowered his hand and opened his eyes. "I sense that you're a Native American," Burroughs concluded. "And as one, you should be more in tune with the power of the spirit world and the good and evil it does for society. But I don't get the feeling that you are in tune."

"*Really?*"

"Yes, Ms. Nightcrow. Native Americans are not as worldly as most. They're naturally proud of their ancestors' simpler ways and their special connection with the spirit world. Truth-be-told, I think that in a way most would rather still live that way. But you don't seem to."

Luna bristled. "Well, I'm sorry if I don't "seem to" share that narrow-minded view of Native Americans, Mr. Burroughs!" she growled.

Tiago finally stepped in. "All right, that's enough!" he said firmly. It was the first time Luna felt Tiago's tough cop persona. "Just like you, Ms. Nightcrow, Mr. Burroughs is here as part of the murder investigation. Like it or not, he *has* been instrumental in helping to close several cold cases for other police departments across the country."

"Even before you showed me your ID, Ms. Nightcrow, I sensed that your presence here was of an investigative nature. And your skin tone and facial bone structure suggested to me that you are Native American and probably from a tribe in the Southwest, am I right?"

"It doesn't take a psychic to see the obvious, Mr. Burroughs," Luna scoffed. "As for "an investigative nature," why else would I be in a burned-out building when there's so much more to do in Miami?"

"The obvious isn't always so obvious. You should know that, being an insurance investigator," Burroughs argued.

"Look, I have better things to do than to shoot the breeze with you, Mr. Burroughs."

"See, Ms. Nightcrow, we both agree on something: I can't spend much time chatting either. Like Detective Toussaint said, I'm here on official business too."

"Ms. Nightcrow, this is a homicide investigation," Tiago reminded Luna: "There is strength in numbers; try to work as part of a team."

"Well put, Detective Toussaint," Burroughs approved. "Teaming up may mean that somebody's got your back."

"Is that to watch or to use as a pin cushion?" Luna asked suspiciously.

Burroughs didn't answer. He turned to Tiago and asked, "Can I borrow your flashlight?"

Luna got a parting jab in. "Why would such an *enlightened* man like you need the guidance of a flashlight?"

Burroughs smirked and waddled off with the flashlight he asked for, leaving Tiago and Luna alone.

"Now what was that all about?" Tiago asked.

"Sorry, detective," Luna apologized, "But Burroughs is one of those guys who makes bank off of stereotypes and superstitions. Just look at him: When's the last time he did any *legwork?* All Native Americans are medicine men who live in teepees—*spare me!*"

"I see what you're saying," Tiago softly sympathized.

"The world revolves around him: He never admits he's wrong about anything!" Luna continued to rant. "Take that missing little boy in Chicago, for example: Burroughs said he was dead. It turned out that he was alive and well! It gave the kid's mother a heart attack. But Burroughs said he meant that the boy was *spiritually* dead, not *physically* dead."

"For a woman who doesn't dig Burroughs, you sure sound like you don't miss a show," Tiago laughed.

"Know your enemy *and* yourself…, detective," Luna paraphrased a line from Sun-Tzu's *The Art of War*.

Tiago was personally impressed, but unmoved in his duty. "He's part of the team, like it or not, Ms. Nightcrow. Like the captain said, manpower's stretched thin. We can use all the help we can get. But look on the bright side, okay? You're pretty much getting free run of this town, to help crack this case."

A town I've only been in for less than 48 hours and know only trivial stuff about, Luna silently scoffed. "All right," she surrendered aloud. "But Burroughs isn't the main reason why I was a bit edgy. Things were a little tense on the ride over here."

"What happened to the calm, cool Ms. Night-crow I picked up from the airport and briefed? You seemed like the type who eats tension on toast and then goes back for seconds."

Tiago's casual cop side calmed Luna again. "Well, the tense situation I ran into earlier was that I think someone was following me from the hotel."

"Well, it wasn't Burroughs; I drove him out here."

"I know," Luna replied. "I called Central and they said you were out."

Tiago took a pen and notepad from inside his suit coat pocket. "You said you were followed, by whom?"

"I couldn't tell what race or gender; the driver's side sun visor was down. But whoever it was did a good job of keeping their distance. I mean, not tail-gating me, but staying a car or two behind. They were well within range the whole drive."

"Did you get a make, model, or plate of the vehicle?"

"It was a white subcompact...probably a two door. It tailed me from the vicinity of the hotel onto Palmway Freeway."

"For how long and how far would you say, Ms. Nightcrow?"

"I-I can't say for sure, detective."

Tiago hadn't written anything yet. He didn't need to, with Luna's scarce description. "You know what this amounts to, don't you?" Tiago cautioned.

"Not even a hill of beans because the description is vague," Luna moaned.

Tiago nodded and changed the subject to the immediate crime scene. "Did you happen to find anything in here that we didn't find already?"

"*DETECTIVE!*" It was Burroughs's voice.

"No, but sounds like someone may have," Luna moaned.

Tiago and Luna moved in the direction of

Burroughs's voice. The space they entered was darker than what they left. So, without a flashlight, the investigators stepped carefully. Tiago made out the beam from the flashlight he loaned Burroughs and led Luna towards its eerie glow.

When they cleared a wall, they saw Burroughs, with head bowed and flashlight in mouth. He held something in his hands; and, as Tiago and Luna got closer, the light revealed that it looked like a dented, warped box.

Tiago asked, "Find something, Mr. ...?"

Burroughs grunted something akin to *"SHHH!"* If Tiago could have seen Luna's eyes, he would have seen them roll. Meanwhile, Burroughs's eyes opened. He removed the flashlight from his mouth and handed it to Tiago. And a triumphant smile filled his face.

"The spirits have led me to believe that this box, though empty, contains information important to this case, detective!" Burroughs concluded. He handed Tiago the piece of debris.

Tiago looked at it, but really didn't know what it was. "Well, thank you, Mr. Burroughs," he finally remarked. Tiago turned the flashlight on Luna and, before she could react, muttered, "Don't worry: Whether it's meat-and-potatoes evidence or fluff, you'll get a taste of whatever forensics cooks-up."

"Not if Burroughs gets to it first," Luna grunted.

CHAPTER TEN

Suspects to Consider

After an hour or so of digging through ashes and soot and finding nothing in Kelvin Frost's place, Luna returned to her car. She was about to leave when she thought about the rest of Riviera Row. The residences were mostly rented. And where would potential renters go for more information? *To a leasing office,* Luna thought. It was another lead, and a reason to stay.

Luna opened the glove compartment and pressed the automatic trunk release button. The lid popped open and she went back to get her laptop and smartphone. Luna walked a block to the leasing office and met with Eunice Crossley: The 72 year-old land lady that Tiago mentioned during the briefing at Central Headquarters.

"I bought this property 2 years ago and moved

down from Bismarck, after my husband died. I probably should have stayed," the grandmotherly Ms. Crossley grumbled.

"*Why?*" Luna asked. "Considering how cold it gets in North Dakota, I'd..."

"Haven't you heard, dear? They've struck oil up there!" Ms. Crossley interrupted. "People are moving up there now the way they used to move to California when I was a girl."

Luna smiled courteously and got down to business. She took out her smartphone and showed Ms. Crossley the downloaded photo of Hector Luz.

"Handsome devil isn't he?" was Ms. Crossley's first reaction to the picture. "But that's not Kelvin Frost. He's too dark—I mean, medium. The Kelvin Frost I rented to was almost white. But the dark hair made him look a little Hispanic: You know, Cuban...*maybe?*"

"Did you ever have any reason to visit his apartment for...maintenance problems, let's say?" Luna asked.

"No, never," Ms. Crossley answered. She folded her arms and looked fondly out the window. "He came down, out of the blue, and asked about renting. I showed him the green apple apartment. It was so hard to lease—maybe because of the color. But, he liked it and paid me 2 months' rent in advance and *in cash*.

"I told the police and now I'm telling you: Nobody complained about loud noises or anything while he was over there. If only all my renters were as good as that Kelvin Frost was."

Luna finally left Riviera Row and returned to The Palm Paradise Suites. She stopped by the hotel restaurant and had dinner. At 5:30 p.m., Luna finally returned to her room. She set her laptop on the desk, undressed, and entered the bathroom. After a long, hot shower, Luna slipped into a short, red satin robe and fired up her laptop again. It was time to fill in Farad back in OKC.

Another check of the online public records databases, combined with a cross-check of the police files, showed that there were only a handful of live Kelvin Frosts in the entire United States. And none of them had life insurance policies with Charmed Life, much less even heard of the company.

So more and more, it looked like the Kelvin Frost from Alabama faked his death and moved to Florida (with hopes of scamming Charmed Life again with a stolen identity and new application). But, he was murdered. If true, Luna saw something encouraging. With human remains this time, to use Kelvin Frost for profit again would immediately set off alarms. Charmed Life could alert their customers and policyholders to be on the lookout for Kelvin Frost fraud attempts.

But there were still three things left for Luna to figure out. First, she had to find out if the character Kelvin Frost was connected to the new application in Miami; second, who killed the real Kelvin Frost; and third, she had to locate Hector Luz.

Though it looked good in her report, Luna wasted time at the actual crime scene. She should have known that the police picked the place clean of any clues. Kelvin Frost's remains were the biggest find, despite Umber S. Burroughs's belief that he found something bigger. But talking with Bekka Noon, Quinn Wu, and Eunice Crossley was productive and gave Luna some suspects to consider.

Bekka was determined to keep the fictitious Kelvin Frost alive for financial gain. Of course, it wasn't a crime to hold on to a dream (in hopes that one day it came true). But Bekka's idea of making it big from a Kelvin Frost book—and a first-time, self-published e-book, at that—was short-sighted. She knew that, and may have settled on creating the more lucrative insurance scam instead. And coincidentally, Bekka's made-up description of Frost (as tall, dark, and "cut") was similar to Shandon Sayers's brief, real-life observation. Though, as Bekka pointed out, hers was simply playing to many women's fantasy man.

Quinn Wu, Frost's other creator, seemed to have forgotten about the fictitious character. But unlike Bekka, Quinn had the computer skills to make Frost convincing. There was a lot of online chatting between Frost and Sayers. And Luna thought about all the cases of stolen identities and how records were frequently hacked and misused to commit crimes. In her mind, she could easily hear the educated, confident Quinn make the smooth pay phone call that duped the elderly Charmed Life customer into revealing his Social Security number.

And then, there was Hector Luz.

With his clean record, experience, and wholesome good looks, Luz could easily stage a successful $50,000 fraud and milk it. He knew about the Alabama case and that the 2-year contestability period expired. He could start the scam again, in a new state and with new information. And Luz also probably knew that while there wasn't a set timeframe for filing a missing person report, normally a full police search wouldn't start for a day or two (in the case of the average adult). So Captain Alexander's decision not to immediately ruin his game meant that Luz had enough time to fly in, whack his accomplice, and skip town. But, from the records Farad provided, there was no motive for Luz to cheat Charmed Life.

Luna visited Eunice Crossley, in order to strengthen the inside job theory she started out with. But it seemed Tiago was right: The land lady's description of Kelvin Frost was too broad (and a bit politically incorrect). Luna showed Crossley Luz's picture with the hope—a long shot hope—that, as part of the new Frost's identity, he rented the townhouse himself. But, Crossley said Kelvin Frost didn't look like

Luz. And even if Luz decided to keep the approximate appearance of the Alabama Frost, by paying a light-skinned Hispanic accomplice to rent the townhouse, well over half of Miami's metropolitan population of 5 million people was Hispanic (in one sense of the word or another). That could make finding the identity of the accomplice probably more difficult than picking the winning Powerball numbers!

As for who killed Kelvin Frost, that was a tough one. Assuming that his murder was even related to the fraud, Bekka, Quinn, or Luz could have done it. Though the police basically ruled them out, Luna wouldn't let go. She couldn't let go, with so few solid clues and leads. They all had the means or motives to set up a scam. But Luna just couldn't picture any of them resorting to murder to cover their tracks. Bekka was too ditzy; Quinn, too academic; and Luz, too promising and...*too cute.*

Luna plunked out the possibilities on her laptop. Then she stopped and laughed aloud, "Well, at least all of this will give Farad plenty to chew on, if not gag on. And the objectivity of the report will maintain my spotless, sterling image as a tireless truth-seeker and fearless free-thinker!"

Yeah, right. Luna thought it best to delete that last bit.

CHAPTER ELEVEN

Suspenseful Swim

Finding out that a Hollywood glory hound like Umber S. Burroughs was snooping around for clues—and doing so with the police's blessings—was bad enough. But now, the glare from Luna's laptop gave her another headache. So she closed it (and her thoughts about the case) for a while.

Luna stretched her arms to the ceiling and drew a deep breath. A long exhale followed. And then a series of snaps, crackles, and pops sounded, as she rolled her neck and worked the kinks out of her shoulders. *Work, work, work!* Luna bitched under her breath. That is what her life amounted to so far.

After 10 years (six as a claims adjuster and four in the field as an independent fraud investigator) Luna Nightcrow finally achieved player status in the insurance game. Farad was right: Her smartphone never slept. Many stressed insurance companies (large and small) called, hoping that she could enlighten them or save them. They usually paid well *if* she succeeded. And with 10 percent of the value of the Cherokee talisman she'd recovered as a reward from her last case, Luna had lots of money. But something from that case came to mind.

Luna remembered that Lobo said, "What good is being rich, if you cannot enjoy it in this lifetime." Though he said it in a different context, maybe he had something. Maybe the money Luna made was enough. Enough for her to think about taking some time off—even retiring—to start the family she always fantasized about in her twenties. But Luna came to her senses and laughed aloud at the thought.

Insurance investigations took Luna away from home often, and sometimes abruptly. And confidentiality agreements wouldn't let her discuss the particulars of some cases. So, if she wanted a husband and kids someday, she would probably have to trade in the sports car, secrecy, and long stints away from home—essentially surrender the life she'd trained and sacrificed for.

For now, Luna rubbed the dreaminess from her eyes, cracked her knuckles, and returned to her report. She finally e-mailed her initial findings to Farad at 7 pm. Then, something new about Hector Luz popped into Luna's mind. *What if he wasn't crooked after all?* Then, like her, he'd left the airport; checked into a hotel; and probably rented a car.

Tomorrow's shaping up to be a busy-busy day! Luna said to herself.

To celebrate the new leads she came up with, Luna decided to visit the hotel swimming pool. Not to flirt or show off, like some women, but to actually swim. She changed into the blue one-piece bathing suit she packed; put on a bath robe; and grabbed a towel. Luna locked up and headed over. Though it was already dark, the outside pool didn't close for another half an hour. When Luna arrived, it was empty: The kiddies and their parents were either in their rooms or out enjoying the plentiful Miami nightlife.

Luna hadn't swam outside at night since high school. She removed her robe and climbed the short diving board. With a bounce, Luna dove straight into the deep end. She broke the surface and swam a few laps under the lights. After about 15 minutes, Luna felt re-energized. Just as she prepared to climb out and towel off, Luna looked back over her shoulder. On the opposite side of the pool—beyond the fence and over the hedges—was a familiar sight. *It was the top of a white car!*

Still wet, Luna jumped out of the pool and hurried across the deck. She could still see the white top. Luna picked up speed, finally reaching the gate. She swung it open, but heard a rumble before getting through. By the time Luna got to the parking lot, the car she thought watched her (and earlier tailed her) was gone.

So much for the celebratory swim! There she stood: In a blue bathing suit, in the middle of a hotel parking lot, looking for a car that wasn't there. *Was Luna losing her mind?* If all those desperate insurance company execs who clamored for her help could see her now! Would they still think of her as competent and seek her services? Maybe as a swimsuit model, if all else failed, Luna hoped. But when she noticed her love handles, she thought maybe not.

CHAPTER TWELVE

A Sickening Feeling

Luna tossed and turned all night. But she managed to awake at the 8 a.m. alarm. A cold shower sharpened her senses. Then Luna dressed for business: Putting on her skirt suit, collared-button down shirt, and heels. She fortified herself with the hotel's complimentary continental breakfast (which, today, consisted of a bagel, a bowl of sweetened cereal, and something to drink).

After breakfast, Luna went outside and looked around the parking lot. She saw a couple of white cars parked; but neither was subcompact-sized. She walked outside the gated lot and along the sidewalk for a look. Nothing fitting what she saw twice before was parked along either side of the street. That didn't mean the small, white car couldn't magically appear again during a drive. But if the driver was smart, he or she would switch cars. Then what could Luna look for?

Luna went back to the hotel and climbed into her rental car. There was no use telling Tiago about the mysterious white car's return. Besides, it wasn't against the law to follow someone, unless Luna could prove that the following party intended to do her harm. Without so much as a license plate number, what could the police do anyway? And with Captain Alexander's hope that Luna would pick up the slack, she couldn't show what might be perceived as weakness. If she did, the show of police support might shift fully to someone like Umber S. Burroughs.

So Luna sucked it up and started out for Miami International Airport. She wasn't about to leave town. Instead, she hoped to arrive at some solid conclusions about....

"*Hector Luz?*" The bright-eyed, teenaged ticket counter clerk asked.

Luna noticed the clerk's name tag. "Yes, Zeo," Luna answered, using his name this time. "I'm looking for airport security information pertaining to Mr. Luz's arrival."

Luna handed the clerk a printout of Luz's information. He looked it over and excused himself. When the clerk returned, it was with a grim-faced, gray-haired lady. Maybe it's his mother—*concerned with my intentions towards her son!* Luna thought to herself. She laughed the silly thought off.

"I'm Marcella Morales, Supervisor. How can I help you?' the grim-faced lady asked.

Luna handed the supervisor her ID. "I'm Luna Nightcrow, independent insurance investigator. The company that I represent is looking for Mr. Hector Luz. I'm working with the City of Miami Police Department as part of an investigation into his whereabouts. Is it possible for me to access your security camera files for the date of Mr. Luz's arrival here?'

"And you're working with the police, concerning this matter?" Marcella asked the same question as her teenaged ticket-taking toady.

"Yes, Ms. Morales. You can call them. Ask for Detective Tiago Toussaint of the Criminal Analysis Team."

"Just a moment, Ms. Nightcrow," Marcella said. She disappeared into an office behind the counter.

It appeared that Marcella *was* going to call the police (either to exercise her authority or to indulge in something besides tiresome ticket confirmations). Or maybe it was because of Luna's unusual name and tan features. It was, after all, the lay of the post 9/11 landscape: Suspicion, derision, and outright distrust of anyone who looked or sounded different. For Luna, though, these were the norm well before several Middle Eastern men hijacked and flew planes into buildings.

Luna cringed from the childhood jokes about her name ("lunatic" and "eating crow"); still being called "an apple" (red on the outside, but white on the inside) by some jealous Cherokees; and the age-old stereotype of Native Americans as bloodthirsty savages. But, she always told herself that it wasn't as bad for her as it was for her grandparents. Being well-dressed and educated usually helped Luna along in life.

"You may want to have a seat, Ms. Nightcrow. We have some magazines over there in our waiting area," Zeo the teenaged ticket counter clerk said.

Zeo's innocence and friendly smile made Luna think that the wait *was* just a formality. So she smiled and moved away from the counter to the waiting area. After about 15 minutes, Marcella returned. And her formerly forbidding face was now flushed with an apologetic smile.

"I'm sorry for the holdup," she said. "But with the Latin American business conference in town, we've been told not to..."

"I understand," Luna politely replied.

"Right this way, Ms. Nightcrow."

Marcella led Luna through one narrow passageway after another, until they reached the airport security center. It was the typical high-tech surveillance set-up: A huge room crammed with computer consoles, camera monitors, and playback machines—all operated by mostly twenty-something techs and supervised by older overseers. Marcella introduced Luna to one of the overseers.

"Ms. Nightcrow, this is Victor Jimenez, Senior Airport Security Analyst," she announced. "Victor, Ms. Nightcrow is working with the Miami police and needs your help. I have to return to the desk, Ms. Nightcrow, but should you need anything more from my department, please let me know."

Luna nodded and Marcella left. The Senior Security Analyst turned to Luna and offered his hand. *"Ma'am,"* he formally addressed her as.

Luna shook Victor's hand and explained *again* what she was looking for. Victor asked her to take a seat. He went to a bank of computers and punched something into a keyboard panel. He pulled a compact disc from a small plastic file cabinet and inserted it into a player on the wall.

After 10 minutes of fast-forwarding through several scenes of passengers entering and exiting various parts of the selected terminal, Victor stopped the CD at Luna's command. "There he is: Hector Luz," she announced.

"Picking up his bags without a problem, it looks like," Victor blankly observed.

Hector gathered his luggage and then vanished in the crowd. "Where could he have gone?" Luna wondered aloud.

Victor offered some suggestions. "One of a dozen other terminals, the bar, or a gift shop, for starters," he replied. "But, if that's the case, you're looking at going through *hours* of surveillance footage, ma'am."

"It's important that I find him," Luna maintained. After a few more frames that didn't reveal where Luz went in the immediate terminal, Luna asked to see the outside security camera footage. "I'd like to see how he left the airport—you know, by car, cab..."

"Yes, ma'am," the Senior Security Analyst responded.

Victor took another trip to the CD cabinet. He found the right CD and popped it into the player. About 20 minutes later, the CD stopped at an overhead picture of Hector Luz waiting outside the airport in one of the many spaces that were usually reserved for taxis and shuttle buses. Luna closely watched vehicle after vehicle drive by. Then a car drove up that caught her eye.

"Freeze, please!" Luna told Victor.

Victor stopped the CD. The small, white car looked like the one that followed Luna on the freeway and spied on her while swimming. But because of the camera angle and glare of the evening lights off the windshield, Luna couldn't get a look at the driver. At her request, Victor enhanced the image several times; but it didn't help. All she eventually saw was Hector Luz get in; and the white car, drive away.

A sickening feeling filled Luna.

CHAPTER THIRTEEN

Sideshow Stroll

Luna personally called Farad Alms with a grave request. Then she called Tiago.

"They're digging up Hector Luz's dental records in OKC," Luna told the detective over her smartphone, as she left the airport.

Tiago knew what that meant. *"That's what the airport security tapes led you to believe?"* he asked, wanting to make sure that this wasn't just a hunch (like the white car chase seemed to be).

"That's what a half an hour of waiting to be personally verified and an hour of watching tapes led me to believe—*yes!*"

Tiago knew it wasn't easy for Luna. So he let her snippiness slide. "Let's hope they don't match the remains found in the apartment, okay?"

"Yeah," Luna sighed. Tiago's hope did little to soothe Luna's sickening hunch that Hector Luz was now a victim of foul play, instead of a fraud suspect.

"Oh, on the box Burroughs found yesterday..."

"*What about it?*"

"Not sure yet: The lab's analyzing it for hair, blood—the usual," Tiago answered. "We may have more to go on, once your company gets us those...*records.*"

"Sure. I'll keep you up to speed, detective," Luna said.

"Likewise, Ms. Nightcrow," Tiago replied.

The line dropped off without either saying "good-bye."

The freeway curved towards plentiful palm trees and parks of manicured, emerald green grass. And below a deck of picture-perfect clouds, blue-and-white-glassed skyscrapers sprouted and then soared above the tree line. Luna was close to Downtown, but not upbeat. Suddenly, she decided to lower the windows, open the sun roof, and throw her cares to the tropical winter wind. The steady, 70-degree breeze was intoxicating; it blew through her hair and carried off some of work's wearing weight. Luna's foot eased off the gas. She gave up the chase of the somber case, and instead let her senses stroll through a sideshow of colorfully-dressed crowds; parakeets' commutes between trees; and the other exotic amenities of Miami, one of America's wealthiest cities.

Wealthiest: The word suddenly got Luna's mental fraud investigation gears moving again. That meant that sight-seeing was over. The insurance investigator had another avenue of approach for finding out about Kelvin Frost. And, it took her back to The Modern Museum of Metaphysics (to pickup where she left off with Bekka Noon).

Luna speed-dialed the museum number en route. She got hold of Sharkie Sayles and asked when a good time to talk with Bekka was. Sharkie placed her on hold. She returned to the line and said to drop by at 4:30 p.m. (after a tour was over). When Luna arrived, the tourists were filing out. She spotted Bekka—this time, wearing a purple tie-dyed dress and with her hair in a bun. It gave her more of a motherly air. But when Bekka finally greeted Luna, it was in her usual whimsical way.

Instead of meeting in her cramped office again, Bekka suggested that Luna talk with her outside (on the patio behind the museum). Sharkie Sayles served them some herbal tea and left to tend to the museum.

"It wasn't easy getting loans to build this museum. Bankers first looked at me when I walked in like I was a three-headed Japanese dragon," Bekka answered Luna's question about how she got started in the business. "I've always been into the paranormal, ancient civilizations—*unexplainable stuff*. Lucky for me that people are more open to the unusual down here—not like back home in Georgia."

Luna picked up on something. *"Georgia,"* she responded to Bekka's home state: "So that's where your accent is from! I thought it might be from Alabama."

Bekka smiled. "I know, Ms. Nightcrow: All us Southerners sound alike."

"Sorry," Luna said. Slipping in the reference to the Alabama Kelvin Frost didn't cause any change in Bekka that Luna could detect. So she shifted gears. "You mentioned "unexplainable stuff," Bekka. Do you ever catch that radio talk show *Under S. something* or other?" Luna asked.

"You mean Umber S. Burroughs," Bekka kindly corrected her. "Sure: I call-in sometimes, when he has guests whose studies I can relate to. I even tried to get on as a guest. I sent his producers a bio and some fliers about the museum. They never got back to me though—not important enough, I guess."

Luna dug deeper. "Do you have a lot of customers, Bekka?"

"Actually, the main tourist stops are quite a few blocks down. I'm always competing with the big museums down there. But when the tourists have seen everything, they trickle up here. So business is good. Of course it could always be better," Bekka replied. "That's why I wanted to get Kelvin Frost made into an e-book. I mean, I sell so many books as it is. But one of my own might really put me on the map. I could maybe make him into an artifact hunter who goes all over the world looking for treasure."

"Like Indiana Jones, huh?"

"Oh, that might look like I was stealing the idea, wouldn't it? Maybe it could be K, as in K-a-y, like a woman. And she goes all over the world looking for treasure."

Luna took a sip of tea. "That's a little better," she remarked. "There aren't too many female treasure hunters out there."

"Well, you see the endless possibilities with this idea, Luna. That's why I want to do something with it," Bekka said.

"Were you surprised that Quinn Wu didn't share your enthusiasm?"

"No. She's got her own career teaching and blogging, you know. But maybe she'll come around later, when the plot's setup and the characters are more solid." Bekka set her tea aside and leaned toward Luna, as if to tell her something private. "Personally, I think this whole thing about the guy with the same name as our Kelvin Frost dying in that fire may have her worried."

"Worried…why?"

"She helped think up our Kelvin. Not as much as me, but…well, she may think that whoever killed the other Kelvin may try to kill her," Bekka said. "And if what you told me the other day is true, the person who did the killing may have found out about our fake Kelvin and used him for the insurance fraud."

"So you went to the police not only out of concern for your character, but because you were afraid that something bad might happen to you, too?"

"Yes," Bekka answered. "The cops said it was probably just a coincidence. But I knew better. I mean, when we created our Kelvin, we checked everywhere in Florida to make sure we weren't using a popular name. Back then, we couldn't find anyone with that name down here. But now, somebody who's really named Kelvin Frost is dead and everybody's asking questions."

Luna set her tea aside and said directly, "And that's where I come in, Bekka. Over two years ago, a Kelvin Frost in Alabama drowned. And the company that I represent paid $50,000. The trouble was that they couldn't find a body. Someone in Miami recently filed another application for life insurance, using stolen information and the rare name Kelvin Frost. I need to find out if the Kelvin Frost in Alabama faked his death and filed again. Or, if he was killed in the fire, I need to find out who may have used *your* Kelvin Frost as the idea for a phony application."

"*Wow!* Now I understand: You're here to sort everything out," Bekka said. "But I don't need to make up a phony application for money."

"Maybe *you* don't, but some of your friends...?"

Bekka dismissed the notion with a laugh. "Like I said, Quinn has plenty of money and people who like her. Why would she do it?"

"Maybe she has family or friends who need money?" Luna speculated.

"Her family came here from The Orient. They had a small business and used everything they made to put her through school. But, she's probably repaid them many times over, with the money she makes now!" Then, Bekka sighed. "I like to think the best about people, Luna, which is probably stupid of me."

"Well, from my side of things, people don't always have others' best interests in mind," Luna replied.

Bekka said that she understood. "Miami is a big city; so, there is crime. There's not as much as there used to be though. But when you run your own business, you do worry about being robbed. It's lucky for me that my boyfriend Horus is around. He used to be a sheriff's deputy, but now he runs his own security company, Darksee Security. He makes sure I'm okay. I joke that with a name like Horus, I'm guaranteed to be safe."

"I don't get the part about Horus's name, Bekka."

"Horus was a multi-purpose Egyptian god. Not only was he the god of the sky, but of war and hunting. I have some Egyptian artifacts on display; and replicas, for sale. So my Horus protects the real Horus's stuff," Bekka reasoned.

"Now I understand," Luna said. *It was Bekka logic.* "Well, Bekka, I appreciate your taking so much time to help me."

"Not at all," Bekka replied with a wide smile.

Bekka walked Luna back inside. Before leaving, Luna stopped in the gift shop. She started on that sideshow stroll from earlier, when a necklace made of wooden, geometric pieces caught her eye. "How much for the necklace?" Luna asked Sharkie Sayles, who worked the cash register.

"Forty dollars," Sharkie answered. "It's made of handcrafted teak wood, Luna, with a genuine brass pendant."

Bekka stepped in. "It's *usually* $40.00. But for Luna, it's..."

"No, no: Forty's fair," Luna said, taking two twenties from her purse. "This is a business, after all, and you have to make money."

Bekka smiled. Sharkie wrapped the necklace up and put it in a celestial-patterned designer bag. Luna waved good-bye and left.

Sharkie looked concerned. She pulled her boss aside and said, "I don't mean to pry, Miss Bekka, but she sure asks a lot of questions. Are you okay with that?"

"Oh, I'm just peachy, Sharkie," Bekka replied. "Luna has to ask a lot of questions: She's an insurance investigator. And as long as I tell the truth, what's to worry about?"

"Well, you be sure and let me know, Miss Bekka, if she asks something that you feel uncomfortable about, okay?"

"You know I will, Sharkie," Bekka said, giving her assistant a re-assuring pat on the shoulder. "I don't know what I'd do without you. Remember, I owe pretty much everything here to you: The website, your business advice, and your..."

Sharkie blushed. "You're too kind, Miss Bekka," she replied.

CHAPTER FOURTEEN

The Operative Word

The next day was Saturday. After an early morning swim, Luna spent time researching the case at the public library. Sure: She could have found out more about Bekka's boyfriend, Horus Hakim, from her laptop's background check access. But, for a while, Luna simply wanted to get out of her hotel room. Of course, she was now in another room, that of the library archives; but it didn't feel as lonely as her Palm Paradise suite. Students studying, librarians shelving and helping, and even the snoring of an occasional vagrant made Luna (a woman submerged in deceit and death) feel among the living.

Then, a call came. And hearing it put Luna back in her depth.

Using the dental records from Oklahoma City, Tiago told Luna that The City of Miami Police's

Medical Forensics Unit identified the charred remains found in the Riviera Row fire as Hector Luz's. Luna immediately e-mailed Farad the news. Now she was guaranteed half of the $50,000 (for finding out what happened to Charmed Life's "best investigator"). The other half, for stopping Kelvin Frost, would be much harder to earn.

There *was* a real Kelvin Frost in Miami after all. He was either the fraudulent policyholder from Alabama who moved to Miami or he was the new applicant (created by scammers with the stolen social security number and the fictitious character name). But in either case, he was difficult to spot. And strangely, it all began to remind Luna of a college astronomy lecture on black holes.

It fascinated her how a black hole is invisible to the naked eye. And that the only way to detect one is by the planets and suns that it sucks in. Now, Luna had to find a similarly hard to see force (Kelvin Frost) and somehow stop him from pulling in more money and causing death, destruction, and distrust.

At 2 p.m., Luna drove 20 miles west of Miami to an unincorporated town called Grassy Knoll. About a mile outside Grassy Knoll were the facilities of Darksee Security, the private security and defense consulting firm run by Bekka Noon's boyfriend Horus Hakim.

The bungalow-styled compound looked rather harmless, with only a radio tower and a satellite dish out front. But there were probably all kinds of hidden surveillance systems on the property. Luna wondered where the buried landmines and machine gun turrets might be because the chain-link fence looked too easy to break through.

Luna rang the intercom at the gate. And on cue, a well-built, buzz-cut young man emerged from the building. He swaggered along the paved path leading to the gate and finally stopped short of opening it. The shiny reflectivity of the man's sunglasses provided Luna with two nice mirrors. She checked herself over. Make-up's still holding up! Luna confirmed. She removed her shades, as a show of submission to what seemed like authority.

"Afternoon, ma'am," the well-built man said.

Luna felt like asking, "How fast was I going, officer." Instead, she put on another show—this time, of ignorance. *Are you Horus Hakim?* Luna pretended not to know.

"No, ma'am, I'm Vargas Kane," the well-built man replied. "Is Mr. Hakim expecting you?"

"I'm Luna Nightcrow," was all Luna would say. But she knew she'd have to come up with more than that...and fast.

"It's okay, Vargie," a deep voice bellowed from behind.

When Vargas Kane turned, Luna glimpsed a muscular, Middle Eastern-looking man in the doorway of the bungalow. "A "Luna Nightcrow" asked for you, Mr. Hakim."

"Let her through," the man identified as "Mr. Hakim" commanded.

Vargas Kane reached into one of the pockets of his cargo pants. He took out a key and unlocked the fist-sized padlock on the gate. The gate swung open, but Vargas Kane's bulk remained. "Sorry, Ms. Nightcrow," he said. "Before anyone goes through, it's standard procedure to check for concealed weaponry. Will you please let me look through your purse, ma'am?"

Luna didn't dare to argue. "That makes sense," she said, handing it over. *"So you're Mr. Hakim's...?"*

"One of his operatives, ma'am," Vargas Kane replied, as he pawed through the purse. He picked out Luna's smartphone and looked at it curiously. "Do you mind if we keep this, until the visit is over? It could be used as a data recording device."

So could my brain! Luna thought. But she said aloud, "Certainly. I understand, Mr. Kane."

Vargas Kane pocketed the smartphone and handed Luna her purse. "Now ma'am, if you don't mind, I have to do a pat-down," he said.

I'll strip down, if it gets me through the gate! Luna thought. She agreed to the search, and spread her arms out on command. Vargas Kane was quick and professional. And when satisfied that she wasn't hiding bullets, bombs, or a bazooka beneath her skirt suit, he thanked Luna and escorted her into the compound.

The interior resembled that of a construction site office, with lots of maps, radios, and other equipment in each room they passed. Vargas Kane led Luna to Horus's office at the end of the hall. Horus sat behind a large desk that had a computer and stacks of neatly-filed papers on it. Luna noticed a paperweight of what looked like an Egyptian pharaoh's head (probably a gift from Bekka). Vargas Kane formally introduced Luna. Horus thanked and then dismissed him. The door shut.

"Have a seat, Ms. Nightcrow," Horus Hakim said. "Bekka told me about you."

"Thank you, Mr. Hakim." Luna pulled up a chair. "Your facility and staff are impressive."

"It seems Bekka was correct in her praise of your discernment. I also value it, Ms. Nightcrow."

"Mr. Kane especially was very professional."

"He is my *right hand*, so the saying goes. I am fortunate to have a man of such high dedication and experience."

Horus was a naturalized U.S. citizen. His wavy hair was as dark as Luna's. Olive-skinned muscles popped and bulged from his black polo shirt. And his clean-shaven, square-jawed face finally flashed a sparkling smile. Luna easily saw why Bekka liked Horus. But, she couldn't clearly see what a hunk like

Horus saw in Bekka. So Luna asked (albeit very delicately).

"Bekka is quite cultured, *for an American*," Horus laughed. "It's nice to see someone take such interest in a culture that is not their own, and then try to get others to appreciate it, too." He patted the pharaoh paperweight affectionately.

As a Native American, Luna silently sympathized. But she stayed on track and asked Horus,"What kind of security do you provide for her?"

"I do not believe it to be proper for me to disclose that information. But, I can tell you that what I do provide for Bekka makes her feel safe. I might also add, Ms. Nightcrow, that it probably makes her feel important, too," Horus said.

"How do you mean?" Luna asked. "With all the collectibles she has, that would be enough to make me feel important."

"But when you are so close to multiple million dollar museums and places for learning in Downtown Miami, I believe that Bekka feels like a small fish—I think is the term—sometimes. I don't want to sound self-important, but for her to have a man who looks like me and who has the capabilities I have, well...."

Luna knew it was true: The tough guy/bad boy image had its appeal. "Like somebody once said, "Power is the ultimate aphrodisiac," Luna added.

"What great leader said this?" Horus asked.

Luna guessed, "Kissinger or Nixon, I believe."

"Wise men."

"Not so wise, *in Nixon's case, at least,*" Luna grunted.

Horus chuckled. "He was caught doing what they all do," he dismissed Luna's reference to Watergate illegalities.

Luna got back to business. "Do your security guards...?"

"We use the term "operative" here, Ms. Nightcrow," Horus firmly corrected Luna.

"I'm sorry. Do your *operatives* drive company or private vehicles during surveillance?" Luna rephrased the question.

"The term is "protective detail"; and we utilize whatever equipment that is necessary to ensure a client's safety."

"Do you happen to own a white car?"

"White is the color of the woman I like, but not the car I drive," was how Horus answered. "White is not good for watching suspicious activity. It is obvious; the criminal can see you too easily. Why do you ask these things, Ms. Nightcrow?"

Luna shrugged, but didn't answer.

Horus sensed Luna's avoidance (though blind to his own). "Well, perhaps I have an answer," he said. Horus's eyes narrowed; his face steeled; and his blood began to boil. "You think that *I* killed this Kelvin Frost, simply because my skin is not the color of the car you asked about, Ms. Nightcrow."

The tension in the room made Luna feel like the walls were closing in. "I'm not sure what skin color has to do with car color, Mr. Hakim," she said.

Horus leaned forward in his high-backed chair toward Luna. "You're not speaking to someone who sneaked into this country yesterday. I know about profiling and trick questioning. So be careful, Ms. Nightcrow."

Horus's radical change in posture and pronouncement rattled Luna. "Is that a threat, Mr. Hakim?"

"No, Ms. Nightcrow. It is just an assurance that I know the games you and the cops play."

Luna gave as good as she got. "Obviously," she replied to Horus: "You were a sheriff's deputy *once*. But some research I did today indicates that you were let go for insubordination."

Horus smirked. "You can rest in comfort with this in mind, Ms. Nightcrow: If the killer comes for Bekka, they will have to fight through *me* to get to her."

"For what it's worth, she's lucky to have someone like you to protect her. I'd like to think that if the killer comes again, you might extend your protective shield around me, too."

Horus didn't reply. He leaned back, sheathed his smirk, and looked at his wrist (which was wrapped in a Rolex). "If you have no more questions for me, Ms. Nightcrow, I have much business to do," he said.

Horus stood and shook Luna's hand. But when he did, he didn't adjust the pressure to accommodate a woman's grip. Horus applied the firm clench of a man-to-man handshake. It was a reminder to Luna of his power, of what he was capable of. Horus let go of Luna's hand and sat down. *"Vargie!"* he snapped.

The door opened, and Vargas Kane stepped into the room. *"Yes, Mr. Hakim?"*

"Ms. Nightcrow is leaving now," Horus said.

Vargas Kane gently bumped Luna's shoulder. She jumped (to the inner delight of Horus). When Luna calmed down, she turned around. Vargas Kane's hand was extended; and in it was her smartphone. "Ma'am," the operative offered.

"Thank you, Mr. Kane," Luna replied. She flashed what she hoped was an appealing smile. But Vargas Kane's icy-blue eyes stared straight forward, awaiting the next order from his boss.

"It seems Bekka was hasty in her praise of your discernment," Horus told Luna.

The insurance investigator's spine stiffened. "And are you going to *talk to her* about that?" she spat.

"With her," Hours emphasized, deflecting the implication of intimidation.

"I'm so glad, Mr. Hakim. A parting bit of advice though: Talk softly, but *don't* carry a big stick."

Horus either didn't recognize or wasn't impressed with Luna's clever twist on Theodore Roosevelt's famous quote. He simply signaled to Vargas Kane, who swept his arm toward the open door. Luna turned and left. When the door closed, Horus

94

pulled up his computer keyboard. He punched in commands and waited. After a moment, a person appeared onscreen. Horus picked up a microphone. "Brett, when you return to base, it is important that you come see me. I may have an assignment for you to carry out," he said.

Meanwhile, Vargas Kane escorted Luna outside. He opened the gate and she walked through. "Ms. Nightcrow," Vargas Kane called. When Luna turned, she noticed that Vargas Kane had removed his sunglasses. The iciness of his eyes and demeanor melted a bit when he told her, "Just so you know, Mr. Hakim has a lot on his shoulders, ma'am." That seemed to be Vargas Kane's way of apologizing for Horus's behavior.

"We all do, Mr. Kane," Luna responded, slipping on her shades. "But thank you for letting me know."

She watched Vargas Kane turn and walk back inside. Once he was gone, Luna got into her car and headed back to Miami.

Back inside the compound, Horus called Vargas Kane into his office.

"Yes, sir?" Vargas Kane asked.

"Do you think Brett is ready for a big assignment?" Horus wanted to know.

"Depends on the assignment, sir."

"I want him to watch over someone and to watch her very well."

"Surveillance, huh? Well then, sure: Brett's all

good. A plain-looking kid like him won't stir up suspicion," was Vargas Kane's assessment of his fellow operative. "I recall that my first Darksee job was surveillance, too, once I left the Navy."

Horus nodded. "And a quality performance you gave, by saving a life," he commended Vargas Kane. "Talk of it gave us many contracts."

"Thank you, sir," Vargas Kane said. "Just stepped up my guarding game. I reckon Brett will do the same."

CHAPTER FIFTEEN

Off Duty Developments

Luna arrived back in Miami at about 3:30 pm. She gassed up the car and returned to the public library to continue researching the case. About an hour later, she left for the hotel. En route, Luna switched the car radio from FM to AM for the 5 o'clock local news. And just like she thought, the story about the misidentification of the Riviera Row explosion victim's remains was a story. But it took a backseat to a more important bulletin: The Miami Dolphins scored some big name free agent signings.

The most exciting thing about the police misidentification for the local reporters was that it not only gave them a mystery to follow, but it also brought in top-name, out-of-town talent (namely Umber S. Burroughs) to solve the crime. Luna turned off the radio before a sound bite from Burroughs played.

She pulled into the hotel parking lot at 5:30 pm. And as soon as she opened the door to her suite, her smartphone rang. "Hello?" Luna answered.

"Ms. Nightcrow, how are you holding up?" It was Tiago.

Luna shut the door and flipped on the lights. "I'm hanging in there, detective," she replied, trying to hide the strain in her voice.

"See the local news?"

"I heard most of it in the car."

"*Most?*"

"Yeah. It seemed like the signal cut-out, just as a wicked wind from the west was about to blow hard."

Tiago chuckled. Then he asked, "Any new developments on your end."

Luna replied, "I have lots of new developments. The question is how much time do you have to hear them all?"

"Well, I have a little vacation time I can put in for, if we need to."

That made Luna laugh.

"Say, how about you tell me over dinner?" Tiago offered. "I haven't eaten anything decent all day."

"Sounds great, but..." Luna hesitated.

"*But what?*" Tiago asked.

"You're not married or committed, are you?" Luna asked with care.

"Married, no; but my mother thinks I should be

committed...*for being crazy enough to join the police!"* Tiago laughed. "And you?"

"I'm married to my job," Luna replied. Then she became serious and said, "Which means I'm committed to catching Kelvin Frost."

"We've always had that in common," Tiago remarked. "Well, since you're paying for dinner, the least I can do is pick you up."

"I'm paying?!"

"You have plenty of expenses; and I'm sure the chamber of commerce would love for you to spend a portion of them on a hotel *and* fine dinning."

Luna remembered her earlier words and chuckled. "I'll gladly take your advice on the right restaurant for the price," she gave-in.

"Deal," Tiago said. "But let's make it 7 o'clock. I have to check-in Downtown and then change."

"Seven it is."

"See you then, Ms. Nightcrow."

"Bye."

Luna tossed the smartphone on the bed. She locked the door and fell softly against it. Her eyes closed and she breathed a long sigh that was a mix of relief and exhaustion. The seismic shift in the course of the case and verbally sparring with Horus Hakim left her mentally worn down. And when the mind goes, so goes the rest.

Luna felt a little like being a girl again—when she played kickball with the boys. Their rough house jabs and punches often didn't adjust to the feminine physique. The cuts, bruises, and barbs always seemed to take longer for her to physically and emotionally recover from.

Tiago's offer of dinner was a nice boost though. It was the first time Luna had the chance to go out on the town *with someone else..* And after a quick, but steamy, shower she felt like changing into something that would really make the evening special. She just hoped that Tiago didn't have burgers and fries in mind for dinner!

A few minutes before 7 o'clock, there was a knock on the door. Luna hurried to the peep hole. She confirmed the identity of the knock's owner, and unlocked the door. The door opened, and so did Tiago's mouth. *"Wow!* That black dress is breathtaking!" he said. It was the response Luna hoped for. "And the necklace..?"

"Chez Bekka."

"Chic."

"And made of teak," Luna added. "I like your style, too. The white linen suit and black shirt remind me of that old TV show *Miami Vice.*"

"Thanks," Tiago laughed. "I wish I had Don Johnson and Phillip Michael Thomas's salaries, too!"

Luna locked her door and followed Tiago to his car, which was a modest, burgundy-colored Buick (instead of the sleek Ferrari Testarossa sports car the TV detectives drove). They strapped in and cruised to a swank Haitian restaurant in the Bayside Marketplace.

Tiago found a patio table with twin torch lights. He pulled out a chair for Luna and took a seat across from her. Tiago ordered dinner in French, and then uncorked the bottle of red wine on the table. He poured Luna a glass and one for himself.

The bay beyond danced with red, blue, and yellow reflections from the festival-colored surroundings. Luna watched white tour yachts glide in and out of port, as a Muzak version of the Marvin Gaye song *Just to Keep You Satisfied* filled the air.

"Miami's a beautiful city," Luna remarked softly. "I said that I wouldn't let it get to me, but…"

"It's okay, Ms. Nightcrow, you're allowed," Tiago laughed. He looked out over the bay with her. "I'm always so busy asking questions and questioning answers that I often forget how lovely this town can be, too."

"The way you spoke French…you're not originally from Miami are you, detective?"

"No," Tiago answered. "I was born in Haiti, hence the French and the restaurant. My family moved to South Florida when I was a teenager. If you know anything about Haiti, Miami is a BIG step up—paradise, practically."

"What made you want to be a cop?" Luna asked.

"In a word?"

"Use two, if you like."

"Stability and respect," Tiago replied. "Some people may not like me personally, but they have to respect the badge and what it stands for. I mean, that's a great feeling: Knowing you have the authority to try and make this a better town for..." Tiago stopped. He realized that it sounded like he was reading from some policeman's book of prepared politically correct answers and laughed at himself. "I know," he said aloud, but really to himself: "Wait until your gut grows and you get some gray in your hair. Then, you'll grow-up."

The waitress brought Tiago and Luna their meals. There were pates, which looked like pitas to Luna; then, "legim" (a thick vegetable stew); next, a spicy coleslaw-like side that Tiago called "pikliz"; and finally, and most recognizable, French bread. Tiago didn't touch his food. Instead he touched upon what was still eating at Luna. "Hey, I'm sorry about Hector Luz," he said.

Luna was sunken in her glass of wine, but surfaced and stiffened. "I didn't know him personally," she said with a shrug.

"But still..."

"Being an insurance investigator's not like being a cop. If we go down, nobody's going to build a statue or a killed-in-the-line-of-duty memorial. No solemn ceremony with fellow investigators pouring in from across the country. Most people dread insurance companies: The salespeople; the premiums..."

"Yeah, but you independent investigators seem

to do all right." Tiago explained to Luna: "You travel, get expense accounts, earn pretty commissions, and everybody pats your back for finding the truth when nobody can."

"You know, I've got this cute little sportscar, a two-seat convertible. But it seems like the only passenger lately has been my ego, my search to secure more and more material, rather than a real man. Guys are so hard to keep, to start a family with. All my success makes them feel like failures."

"Don't sell yourself short," Tiago remarked. "Those kind of guys aren't worth staying the night with, and especially not forever with."

"I know, detective. But when someone else has a lot … I mean, I've been jealous like that too."

"You wouldn't be human, if you weren't."

"When I was brand new to the independent investigating side of the business, I loved the hunt. The legwork was great for the calves. But now ..?" A sigh slipped from Luna's lips, as she returned to the present. "Well, at least confirmation of Luz's death does focus the investigation."

For a while, Tiago forgot that he invited Luna to talk about the case. "So, Ms. Nightcrow," he said, adjusting his chair, "tell me more about K-Fraud."

The First Move

"K-Fraud," Luna laughed. "I like it."

"Sounds like a gangsta rapper. But it's all yours."

"Well, Bekka's a sweet lady, even though she's not quite dealing from a full deck," Luna continued.

"Tell me about it!" Tiago groaned, unfolding his napkin and draping it over his lap.

"But her boyfriend, Horus Hakim, seems to have his act together: Brawn, brains, and a private defense consulting company that, from all reports, is above board."

"You're not going McDreamy over him are you?"

Luna made a silly face. "No," she answered. "Horus isn't perfect: He has a temper. He got hot over some questions that he thought were racial profiling. Being Cherokee, though, I can't say that I blame him."

Tiago washed down his *legim* with some wine.

"You were just doing your job," he said. "Besides, some of those independent defense contractors can be tough—*very tough*."

"So am I; I got out of there alive, didn't I?" Luna said. "Horus may have overplayed his hand though. One of his *operatives*, as he calls them, seemed to apologize for his boss's macho performance."

Tiago grinned. "So you made a friend in the lion's den after all, huh?"

"Friend is too strong a word, detective."

"What about Quinn Wu: Get anything from her that we didn't?"

"She's bright..."

Tiago cut a piece of *pate*; and then, to the chase. "Bright enough to use her computer skills to create an online scam involving Kelvin Frost and use it over and over for financial gain?" he asked.

"You knocked that one out of the park, detective."

Tiago grinned. "Please let the Miami Marlins know. They need home run hitters, and I could use some extra money. Seriously though, Ms. Night-crow, the only trouble with that theory about Wu is that the woman's a tenured prof. Add to that, her blogging biz on the side rakes in more money. She's got her head screwed on straight enough. So what would be Wu's motive for committing fraud?"

Luna sighed. "Bekka said the same thing."

"Well, even a broke clock's right twice a day," was Tiago's back-handed way of giving Bekka her due.

"There are a few more things I'd like to check out," Luna said.

"Like Burroughs?"

"I wasn't going there."

"Yet, you mean?" Tiago asked.

Luna grunted, "I've never bought into that psychic stuff."

"What about a woman's intuition?"

"That's totally different! How can generations of women be wrong about a totally unscientific source of feminine power?"

"I sense sarcasm," Tiago teased.

"A heaping helping of it, detective!" Luna added, spreading some *pikliz* on a piece of bread.

"Well, for what it's worth, I like your company better than Burroughs's."

Luna stopped eating. She saw an opening to take things where she hoped they might naturally go. "Is that on or off the record, detective?" she asked Tiago.

"On," he said. "Who wants to be friends with someone who can read your mind?"

"Oh." Luna sloshed the last sliver of wine in her glass. She lifted it to her lips and tipped it in. "I thought there might be *another* reason why you like my company."

"Something like Burroughs isn't as stunning as you?" Tiago offered. "Well, someone said the other day that "it doesn't take a psychic to see the obvious.""

Luna came out with it. "I don't think I've *ever* seen anyone like you, Tiago," she bubbled over.

There was a long pause. Luna dared to look deep into Tiago's dark brown eyes. And when he looked into hers, he noticed that the color and intensity mirrored his own. Luna decided to make the first move, and reached across the table to touch Tiago's hand. And while he didn't stop her increasing caress, his eyes looked down. And suddenly, the detective looked out of it.

"Luna—I-I mean, Ms. Nightcrow..," Tiago stammered.

Once that happened, Luna didn't feel the warmth she thought she would from him. She remembered the tingle she felt from Tiago's casual, confident air and when he paid attention to what she said. *And, oh: The French!* All of that should have been enough. Now, Luna knew it would have to be enough.

She reminded herself that they were both criminal investigators: Cynical and clinical by nature. They'd seen the many ways people used words and deeds to achieve an end (usually, a criminal one). So they vowed publically and privately not to let themselves be so easily conned, by vetting, verifying, and watching every action or inaction.

The rest of the dinner was spent doing what is normally done at dinner: Just eating and drinking.

CHAPTER SEVENTEEN

Too Much At Stake

Luna and Tiago arrived at The Palm Paradise Suites around 8:30 pm. They parked, but neither left the car. Tiago finally looked at the passenger side. "Luna," he began to say, in a tone that she heard too many times lately, "I hope I didn't mislead you into thinking that dinner meant…"

Luna shook her head 'no.' "I know, Tiago: There's too much at stake. This has to stay professional," she said softly. "It's just that, well, I've been working a lot lately—maybe too much—and…" Luna stopped herself. She simply replied, "I'm sorry I let my guard down tonight."

Tiago smiled. "We're all human," he gently reminded Luna. "We all have to take a breath—a pause from the cause. Even I took one tonight, by wearing *this* outfit. Leaving my apartment, I thought I might get busted on a 314."

"A three-fourteen?"

"Indecent exposure," Tiago said straight-faced.

Luna couldn't conceal a chuckle. But her smile turned upside down at the abrupt ringtone of a smartphone. It was hers, *of course.* "Hello?" Luna answered.

"Hi, Luna. I didn't catch you at a bad time, did I?" It was Quinn Wu.

Luna's eyes widened with surprise and her toes tapped with anticipation. "No, no, of course not, Quinn," she stammered.

Quinn sounded concerned. "I saw the local news online tonight. They're reporting that the man killed in the explosion wasn't named Kelvin Frost."

"That's right."

"I did some digging and I found something that may help your case. Can you come over?"

"*Sure!* Give me a minute to find a pen and paper." Luna snapped her fingers in Tiago's direction. He searched his pockets for a pen, and found one. Luna supplied a napkin from her purse and proceeded to write down Quinn's address. Luna thanked her and hung up. "Thanks for the pen," Luna told Tiago.

Tiago made a face. "One has the Pen; and the other, paper. We might make for one heck of a tag-team!"

"Or as a nursery rhyme, if this case doesn't get solved," Luna said. "I got my wish: That was Quinn Wu. She says she has some information."

"Where to, Ms. Nightcrow?" Tiago asked, ready to turn the key.

Luna's instincts caused her to hesitate. This was *her* lead. But she remembered what Tiago said earlier about sharing whatever she cooked up. So she decided to let the police in on the hunt and read Tiago the address. The ignition started and Luna and Tiago raced away.

CHAPTER EIGHTEEN

An Unexpected Turn

It was after 9 p.m. when Luna and Tiago pulled into the well-to-do section of The Upper Eastside neighborhood. The car turned onto the street where Quinn Wu's white, Spanish-styled house was. An iron fence surrounded the residence. But it appeared that Quinn left the main gate open. So Tiago drove through. Outside, the hanging lantern porch light shone. And from inside the house, what looked like a living room light was on. Tiago parked his Buick next to a black Audi that was probably Quinn's. Luna got out, but the detective didn't.

Puzzled, Luna looked back through the passenger side window. "You're not coming in?" she asked Tiago.

"I don't want to scare Wu," he explained.

"Do you mean with your badge or your outfit?"

"I thought you liked the outfit!"

Luna smiled playfully and started off for the house. When she got there, she noticed that a wrought iron storm door guarded the main entry. So instead of knocking, Luna rang the doorbell. There was no answer. Luna rang a few more times; but still, no one answered. After an unsuccessful knock on the wrought iron door, Luna took her smartphone from her purse and re-dialed Quinn Wu's number. Tiago watched what was going on. He saw Luna eventually return to the car.

"*Well?*" Tiago asked.

"No answer from the doorbell or cell," Luna replied.

Tiago instinctively pinned his badge on his belt and opened his glove compartment. He took out his belt holster and back-up weapon, a blued steel .38 caliber revolver. Once set, he left the car and joined Luna. The two walked the path that led to the house. Luna returned to the front door, while Tiago left and snooped around the front of the house. The exotic shrubbery and awnings above the front windows made it difficult to get a clear peek inside. But from what Tiago could see, nothing looked unusual in the living room.

"*Detective!*" It was Luna's voice calling. Tiago hurried over. When he got there, he noticed that Luna held the wrought iron door open.

"How did..?"

"I just turned the handle and it opened," Luna interrupted.

Tiago extended his arm and signaled for Luna to move aside. She did, and the detective drew his revolver. He re-opened the wrought iron storm door and turned the doorknob on the front door. It was unlocked, too. Tiago entered the house first. Luna followed. There was a shadowy hallway that branched off into different rooms. The only one that was lit seemed to be the living room. *"Ms. Wu?"* Tiago called. There was no answer.

Luna closed the front door gently. Tiago moved down the hall. Luna caught up, and both stopped before entering the living room. Leading with his revolver, Tiago inched his way in. And what he saw looked like the aftermath of a hurricane, with papers and trash strewn across the floor. Luna noticed a computer terminal in the corner. Its screen was black and the tower was smashed.

Suddenly, there was a noise. Tiago spun in the direction he thought it came from—his gun ready. Through the darkness of the next-door room stepped a familiar figure.

"What the..?"

Before Tiago could finish, Luna gasped, "Umber Burroughs!"

Burroughs instinctively raised his hands in the air. "Good evening, Detective Toussaint and Ms. Nightcrow," the celebrity psychic calmly replied.

"Where's Quinn Wu?" Tiago wanted to know. Burroughs didn't reply. He inched a raised hand in the direction of the dark room instead. Tiago caught the move, cocked his gun, and lined the barrel up with Burroughs's belly. "Keep your hands where I can see them!" the detective shouted.

Burroughs begged, *"Don't shoot me, bro! Don't shoot!* I'm just going to turn on the light, okay?" Tiago nodded. The psychic reached his hand around the corner. He flipped a switch and chandelier light showed. It was a dining room. And slumped over the dining room table was the body of a bruised and battered Quinn Wu.

Luna was shocked by the sight. It was an unexpected turn of events. *"Oh my God, detective!"* she cried. Tiago holstered his gun, and then tried to console her. Luna pushed away. Grief wasn't the reason for her outburst; it was urgency. "We have to get out of here!" Luna warned.

Burroughs looked confused. "Why, Ms. Nightcrow? Wu's..."

"Dead—yes! And we could be, too! Because if Quinn was beaten to death, like Hector Luz was, then maybe the killer also turned on..."

Tiago knew what she meant. "Everybody out of the house, now—*now!"* the detective shouted.

CHAPTER NINETEEN

Diplomatic Approach

The police and crime scene investigators soon covered the area and combed the premises for clues. And a pack of TV, radio, and newspaper mutts grew restless outside the gate, with their stomachs growling for a feast of official statements to be fed to them.

Despite Luna's fears, the gas wasn't rigged to blow-up the house. Had she thought about it, Burroughs wouldn't have been breathing when they arrived (if gas filled the house in the quantity necessary to trigger an explosion). As for Burroughs, Tiago pinned him down with questions. And the psychic had answers—*long answers.*

"Remember that burnt box I found in the Riviera Row townhouse that blew up?" Burroughs asked Tiago.

"Uh-huh," Tiago responded blandly.

"I sensed that it might be important to the case, right?"

"Yes, Mr. Burroughs."

"Okay. Most of today, I did more meditation. And it came to me that the half melted plastic box was in fact a CD file case. Compact discs—their shape and size—made me think about what you put them in: A DVD or CD player. And what are these players? Computers, basically! And, after putting the CD container together with computerized playback machines, I sensed that someone would contact me regarding the importance of computers in the Kelvin Frost investigation.

"I was having dinner tonight with an associate when I got a call from Quinn Wu. She said she had something important she wanted to show me. I took a cab up here. The gate was open, the lights were on, and Wu's car was out front. She even left the door open; so, I came in. I found her dead. But like a responsible citizen, I called the police..."

"And the media, too?" Tiago asked.

"Absolutely, detective! *Them's my peeps*, so to speak. I don't forget where I came from," Burroughs shamelessly replied. "Then you and Ms. Nightcrow arrived about 10 minutes later. Now think about it, Detective Toussaint: If I was the killer, would I have stayed around and called the police and the news? I came to Ms. Wu's house tonight at *her* request.

Check her cell phone records and mine to verify who called who."

"No one is accusing you of anything, Mr. Burroughs," Tiago replied.

Burroughs breathed a sigh of relief. *"Good!"* he said.

"But, while you're helping with the Kelvin Frost investigation, *this* homicide is a separate case that you haven't officially been approved to assist us in. And if you called the news because you thought there was a connection with the Frost case, there is no actual proof so far that the two cases are related."

Burroughs hadn't quite thought of it that way. But Tiago gave him an opening that he proceeded to try and shoe horn his big ego through. "Even though I'm not the killer, Ms. Wu invited me here. I found her body and called the police. So it does make me a part of this homicide, Detective Toussaint. And you're aware of my record of success with other law enforcement agencies in similar cases. So..."

"So, Mr. Burroughs," Tiago interrupted, "we would like to ask you to come to headquarters to verify a few more things and..."

"And then talk more about getting official approval for my assistance in this case?" Burroughs asked anxiously.

"That is a possibility."

"Then I'm all yours, detective!" Burroughs announced. "Just let me phone my producer and tell her that she may have to do a Loch Ness

Monster re-run tonight, instead of a live show." Tiago motioned to two uniformed officers, and they escorted Burroughs from the living room.

Tiago walked outside for the first time in 30 minutes. He breathed a sigh of relief and grinned at the success of his diplomatic approach. It got Burroughs out of his hair; and, he hoped, it would keep Luna from pulling hers out. Tiago noticed that Luna returned to his car. He went over and leaned through the open driver's side window.

Luna looked over from her passenger side seat and said, "If you're here to check on me, detective, I'm all right. I've seen dead bodies before."

Tiago grinned. "It's not about you," he said, "it's about that coat you're wearing. Just wondering where you got it; I'd like to get me one to go with my pants."

Luna flashed a faint smile. She pulled the white linen jacket Tiago loaned her for warmth around her shoulders, as a chilly, late night breeze blew through.

"Thanks for the heads-up on the gas," Tiago said.

"That was no "head's-up"," Luna mocked. "It was me losing my head!"

"But not your heart, Ms. Nightcrow," Tiago replied. "If you were right, but said nothing, we could have lost our lives."

Luna nodded absently.

"Well, I took down Burroughs's version of what

happened here. He says Wu called him up here, too. Off the record, I don't think he's the perp."

"Of course not: *He's part of the team,*" Luna scoffed.

"Give me a break, will you!" Tiago groaned. "He called the news, hoping to score. But I told him there's no proof that this is related to K-Fraud. We'll have to check his alibis and clear him, before he even gets a taste of this case."

"But, if what he says is true about Wu's cell phone call..."

"Please, Ms. Nightcrow."

"I know, I know: He's got "free run of the town," too," Luna used Tiago's earlier words.

Tigao took one of Luna's lines. *"You hit that one out of the park,"* he grunted.

Luna recognized what she said over dinner. A soft smile ensued. "You give as good as you get, detective," she said.

Tiago returned Luna's smile with one of his own. But it quickly vanished, when the wail of a departing ambulance siren brought him back to the crime scene. "We'll pick through Wu's computer for more clues," Tiago said. "You're free to come down and take a look at what we get, you know."

Luna nodded, but not at Tiago's offer. Her chin hit her chest, as she *nodded off* to sleep. "Looks like nighty-night for Ms. Nightcrow," Tiago laughed. He climbed in and started up the car.

CHAPTER TWENTY

Roadblock Run

The drive back to The Palm Paradise Suites was quiet. But, it wasn't long enough for a restful sleep. Soon, the car stopped. "We're here," Tiago called softly. Luna woke-up and dragged herself from the car. "Get some sleep, Ms. Nightcrow!" the detective told her.

Luna made a salute. She mumbled, "Yes, sir," and trudged toward the side door.

Luna suddenly realized that she was still wearing Tiago's coat. She looked over her shoulder to see if he was gone. But her head stopped halfway when her eyes picked up on something. Someone sat over near the pool. Nothing unusual, except that the person sat in a small, white car! And when that someone saw that Luna was tuned in, it was time to get out.

"*TIAGO!*" Luna shouted. The detective's brake lights blazed red and the Buick backed up. The white car's engine roared, forcing its screeching tires forward.

The white car driver zoomed around the rows of parked cars. The last lap was a straight shot to the exit. But, Tiago saw the white car coming and spun his Buick around sideways, turning it into a flashing roadblock. The exit was now sealed-off. But, that didn't bother the white car driver: *The car sped-up!* Tiago drew his revolver. Through the open passenger side window, the detective took deadly aim at a pair of oncoming headlights.

But before the driver could bulldoze the Buick out of the way, another car backed out just in time. Luna blindsided the speeding white car, turning it sideways into another vehicle. The impact crushed the car's front end; and with it, the driver's hope of escape.

Tiago barreled out of the Buick. Luna climbed carefully from the Ford Focus. Tiago raised his revolver and crept through the steam that hissed from the white car's busted radiator. He reached the driver's side window. And through gun sights, the detective saw the lone occupant's face buried in a billowy airbag. Carefully, Tiago reached in and felt for a pulse. He found one; then, turned off the ignition; and finally breathed a sigh of relief.

When the situation looked safe, Luna rushed over. Tiago turned around. "You okay?" he asked.

"Yeah," Luna panted. "But the rental car..."

Tiago saw the back end damage and said, *"I hope you took the insurance."*

Luna didn't catch the joke. She was too intent on seeing who the driver of the white car was. When she finally looked inside, she still didn't know.

But Tiago did, and holstered his gun. "Luna Night-crow," he announced, "meet Mr. Jorge De Martine."

CHAPTER TWENTY-ONE

Player Hater

It was 2 a.m. when Jorge De Martine came to...*in a hospital bed.* The young man felt his forehead and realized it was plastered with a bandage. The next thing Jorge noticed was that he had company. But, it wasn't the kind he particularly cared for: A police detective and the woman he'd followed and watched.

Jorge glimpsed a uniformed officer leave the room. And when the door shut, Jorge's mouth opened. "I did not know you, Detective Toussaint!" he shouted. "I would stop if I know, *hombre!*"

Tiago tried to calm him. "Jorge, we want to ask you some questions. You can have an attorney..."

"¡No reconocí a usted, detective!"

"Entiendo," Tiago replied. *"Pero usted reconozca otras personas—esta mujer, por ejemplo. Dinos por qué, Jorge."*

Jorge eased back in his bed. He breathed hard before letting loose with, "I don't have nothing now: I live in my car!" That didn't seem to sway Tiago or Luna. So, Jorge told what he knew (the best he could). "No lawyer; I talk to you, Detective Toussaint. I tell you like when I tell you *nada* about *Señor Frost*, because I no see him. After I tell you, a big, black *hombre*, Burroughs from Cali, want me to tell him about Frost. And I tell him like I tell you—*nada*. But he say he give me money, if I help him."

"*Help him do what?*" Tiago asked.

Jorge pointed at Luna. "To look for her," he said. "Burroughs say she—I mean to say you, *señorita*— was from Frost's insurance company. And you have maybe a reward. If I look for you and go with you, Burroughs say he share the reward with me. *Bueno*, I say. But, I say I need some money now, so my car can be fix."

"Where were you tonight between 8 and 9 o'clock?" Luna asked.

"Eating," Jorge said. "Burroughs take me to a Cuban place. He give me money for gas, and he go. He had to talk to…"a source", he say."

"Did he say who "the source" was?" Tiago asked. "No."

"Did you ask, Jorge?"

"No, detective, I do not want to maybe make him mad, after he give me some money now."

"So you didn't drive Burroughs to "the source's" place in your car?" Luna asked.

"No, *señorita*: Maybe he take him a cab. Burroughs no look like he take the bus or the Metro, *comprendes?* So, I get gas and go to the hotel, *señorita.* I see your car, but no lights I see in your room. They close pool; so, I think you maybe sleep or was eating at some place. So, I just sit to see you come back." Jorge looked across the room, toward something distant. Then he sighed, *"Detesto gastar dinero en mi coche. Constantemente me quejo del precio de la gasolina y los neumáticos. Pero ahora la situación ha cambiado: Vivo en mi coche. Mi coche me cuida ... bueno, hasta anoche. Ahora, mi coche está destrozado. ¿Dónde voy a vivir? Mi vida es un desastre."*

"*¡Cálmate!*" Tiago said. "*Te lo prometo, Jorge: Nosotros le ayudaremos si nos ayudas.*"

"*Gracias,* Detective Toussaint," Jorge replied, with some semblance of a smile starting to show.

Tiago and Luna left the room. Tiago stopped to instruct the uniformed officer posted outside. Then he joined Luna at the elevator and the two entered.

Luna asked about Jorge's drifts into Spanish. "What was that last part about?"

"Just more about him living in his car," Tiago replied. "I think I told him that if he helped us, we'd help him."

"*Think?*"

"If only he spoke French or Creole, I'd of nailed every word," Tiago sighed.

Luna smiled. Then she turned serious. "If what De Martine told us is true, I'd say that this takes

Burroughs from being a team player to being a player-hater."

"Maybe so," Tiago said. "For once, Burroughs isn't the big man. With your sizeable skills and status, you can close this case before he does. Kind of flattering that Burroughs has to spend the time and money to keep up with you, don't you think?"

"Thanks, detective," Luna replied. "But I think this is how he gets most of his supposedly spiritual revelation: By human observation. Super psychic *my ass!*"

Tiago grinned. Then he became serious. "When Jorge gets better, he could be looking at anywhere from 1 to 5 years probation or jail time for resisting arrest."

"Why not tack on twenty-to-life?"

"You mean for maybe driving the white car at the airport that picked up Hector Luz?"

"Bingo, detective," Luna replied.

"We'll ask him about that, too, and have forensics go over every inch of the surveillance tapes you looked at for a matching license plate. But if De Martine's in the game, he's a bit player. You saw how scared he was: He told us whatever he knew. De Martine's an ex-con, but I don't think he's capable of murder."

Luna's jaw dropped. "Even after what happened in the hotel parking lot?!" she asked.

Tiago sighed. "I hear you, Ms. Nightcrow," he

admitted. "Maybe he would have stopped sooner...*if you hadn't backed into him.*"

Luna could see that Tiago was trying to keep De Martine in a cooperative mood. So she calmed down. "Yeah, I was doing my make-up," Luna played along. Then she got back on track. "The white car at the airport: Maybe Burroughs borrowed it from De Martine?"

"Burroughs flew in from L.A. a day after the blast. We were questioning Jorge when he got here. At best, Burroughs hit him up for surveillance duty after we cut him loose," Tiago said, dampening Luna's implication that Burroughs killed Luz. "Besides, Jorge's alibis for his whereabouts before and during the explosion checked out."

"Then how many other drivers of white cars are there in Miami?" Luna asked rhetorically.

"Almost as many as there are people who *look Hispanic*," Tiago said, referring to the vague description of Kelvin Frost. "And even if it is Jorge's car on tape, his lawyer would argue that maybe he loaned it to Burroughs. And then..."

"Burroughs will say that he loaned it to some other flunky who's familiar with Florida, and finger him for the dirty deed. *Shit!*" Luna cussed at the complexity.

The elevator door opened, and Tiago and Luna left the hospital lobby. They went to the car, where the conversation continued.

"Poor Jorge," Tiago sighed. "Not out more than a month and he's probably going back in."

"But if he cooperates, the D.A. can cook up some kind of deal, right?" Luna asked.

"We'll see," Tiago replied. "Maybe we can ask for probation. Jorge pretty much told us everything related to tonight. If it's true, it knocks Burroughs down a peg or two. The D.A. might consider that community service, *on Jorge's part.* She's not a big Burroughs fan either."

"But Burroughs will use his celebrity and that spirit guide stuff to skate by!" Luna snarled.

"Or, he'll get real world legal guidance that will argue that Jorge overstepped the authority he was given," Tiago said. "But, if Burroughs paid a petty ex-con to spy, it's not a stretch to think that he could have hired a pro to do a more thorough, less obvious job: Like planting a bug, for example. Burroughs is maybe deeper into this than we thought."

"He's in it, but not for the insurance money," Luna reluctantly admitted. "Burroughs has money and fame to burn. If he kills someone, it's all gone. But covering a murder investigation brings more. Bekka listens to him and said she calls in. When she called the producers of the show about being a guest, they took down her information. While they didn't book her, Bekka's story about making Kelvin Frost into an e-book with Quinn Wu and the kooky museum probably sparked Burroughs's memory. He read the news about K-Fraud; smelled a show; and set-up shop down here. Maybe Burroughs called Quinn Wu earlier and asked when a good time to stop by was. She called tonight and he used it as the usual *inspiration* to get involved again."

"We've got the muscle to keep Burroughs from bothering you," Tiago said. "After questioning, we'll keep him busy with some dead-end leads."

"Bermuda's not too far off. Why not fly Ouija board boy straight into The Triangle?" Luna suggested. "Lots of *dead ends* there, I understand."

"You're buying the ticket?"

"With my expenses, I could probably buy the plane!"

Tiago chuckled, "You never miss anything do you, Ms. Nightcrow?"

"Only the identities of a killer and a con artist," Luna yawned. "Add a good night sleep to that too, detective."

CHAPTER TWENTY-TWO

Busy-Busy

Luna didn't get a good night sleep. After a few hours of tossing and turning and drifting in and out, she woke at 8 am. A cold shower swept away the sleepiness and most of the soreness from the wreck. Luna put on more make-up than usual. Then she tied her hair in a pony tail; threw her suit coat over a white T-shirt; and wiggled into jeans and flats. When she looked in the mirror, she thought she looked pretty damned good (considering last night's events).

For the better part of the morning, Luna busily squared away the damage done to her temporarily impounded rental car. And with the police sweeping her suite for any traces of bugs or taps, she couldn't go back to the hotel.

While trying to hail a cab, Luna suddenly remembered something about Quinn Wu's house: It had an iron fence around it. Back in Oklahoma City, there were plenty of gated communities, too.

That meant that there was some level of security for these often affluent areas. Luna wondered if Quinn's house had a security system or patrol. When Luna got a cab, she had the driver drop her off at the public library. Inside, Luna spent a couple of hours doing online research about Miami's many additional security firms. She noticed that Darksee took away a few profitable contracts from them, thanks to a heroic Vargas Kane assignment that saved a young Jamaican girl from drowning. "A fellow swimmer," Luna took note of another of Vargas's qualities. She then laughed to herself, *Maybe we could do an underwater ballet someday.*

But taking away business from a competitor almost always causes their feelings to be hurt. Maybe it led a firm or two to relieve the pain of their purloined pay and punctured pride with some soothing revenge. Luna decided to call Quinn's neighbors in the Upper Eastside for more information on their security details: Their hours of operation, operatives' temperament ... the usual background run-down.

At about 3:30 pm, Luna caught another cab. She rode to Central District Headquarters to sift through the evidence taken from Quinn Wu's house and from her South Shore office. Tiago met Luna at the front desk, where he gave her a visitor's badge. She clipped it to the pocket of her suit coat and signed in. Tiago held the elevator, and the two headed up to the Computer Forensics Lab.

"I didn't expect you to take me up on the offer to look through the crime scene evidence so late in the day, Ms. Nightcrow," Tiago laughed.

"I've been busy-busy," Luna replied. "I surfed the Web and called around about the security detail for Quinn Wu's place."

"And you found out that they weren't provided by Darksee Security," Tiago replied instinctively.

"Darn, detective, you spoiled all my fun! Here I had another possible suspect or two, and you've already ruled them out!"

Tiago chuckled. "Don't worry, Ms. Nightcrow: No one's "ruled them out" yet. It's just that there are more immediate suspects to consider—friends, family, or co-workers with an ax to grind."

Of course! Luna realized. She rubbed her eyes. "I'm sorry, detective: I only got a few hours of sleep," Luna sighed.

"For the record, you still sound sharp and look sharp," Tiago replied sympathetically.

Luna smiled warmly at Tiago. She wanted to return his compliment with one of her own, but the level indicator light stopped on three. There was a *ding,* and the elevator doors parted. Tiago and Luna stepped out and into a long corridor. And with other officers passing to and fro, Luna returned to business. "Get anything more from Burroughs?" she asked Tiago.

"He rolled pretty much the way I thought he would," the detective replied. "Burroughs said that hiring Jorge was just a way to verify that his findings jibed with his spirit guides' revelations. And that though he tried to help Jorge, by giving him a few bills, he "didn't intend for him to obstruct justice." Burroughs's vision about the box he found at Riviera Row turned out to be true: *It was a CD container.* But it was so badly damaged that there was no way to lift any fingerprints or extract DNA information. It was in what used to be K-Fraud's living room."

"Find any bugs or taps at The Palm Paradise Suites?"

"No. Your laptop and suite are clean. And we verified that Wu called Burroughs, though there's no evidence that they personally met or talked before then."

"So Burroughs didn't get any further info on K-Fraud from Wu, but they did talk about meeting last night?"

Tiago gave Luna a confirming nod. "The medical examiner's doing the autopsy on Quinn Wu tomorrow," he told Luna.

"What about her computer, her files?" Luna asked.

Tiago picked up on Luna's anxiousness. "They're still analyzing them. There's a lot to go through; so patience, Ms. Nightcrow, patience," he gently advised.

The two walked down the corridor until they

reached a gray door with the sign "Computer Forensics Lab" on it. Tiago took a computerized security card from his suit coat pocket and scanned the electronic lock. After a moment or two, there was a buzz; and then, a 'thud.' Finally, the heavy metal door to the Computer Forensics lab automatically swung open.

Tiago threaded Luna through the maze of cutting edge deciphering machinery. They stopped at a desk where a well-dressed Japanese lady sat poring over her computer console. On a couple of tables next to her were two additional computers: One badly damaged and the other fully functional.

"Luna Nightcrow, meet Nicole Takamatsu, Deputy Chief Analyst," Tiago introduced the young lady.

Luna shook Nicole's hand. "Well, despite the perp's best intentions to destroy evidence, we were able to recover some preliminary information from the victim's computers," Nicole announced. She motioned to the wrecked computer first. "From the damage done to the home computer, it looks like the perp either took a hammer to the tower or simply picked it up and tried to slam it to pieces."

"Any fingerprints?" Luna asked.

"The victim's and a few others that don't match anything in the local, state, or federal crime databases," Nicole replied. "They could be from a repair tech who fixed the computer or from a salesperson at a store where the victim bought the computer from."

"Then it's a dead end on the print ID," Luna sighed.

"We're still on the trail though," Nicole said confidently. "It seems that the perp apparently didn't know that data can still be recovered in some quantity from a computer's hard drive. A computer never really erases deleted data. So unless you junk the whole computer or have some serious encryption protection going, we can still dig up some of the data on the hard drive. What we recovered from the victim's home computer was mostly a lot of digital photos. A couple of files we simply can't crack the encryption on."

"On the photos: We're going through them to see if any familiar faces turn up," Tiago added.

"Did you recover any information from the school computer?" Luna asked.

"That's where things get interesting," Nicole answered. She fed a frenzy of commands into her keyboard and waited. A few seconds later, the computer screen displayed some of what the lab was able to preserve. "Aside from a lot of blogging data, teaching tools, and other material relevant to the victim's profession, so far we've turned up several visits to public records databases. And there was a lot of data on IRS regulations, the National Crime Information Center, EIN..."

Luna picked up on something. *"Wait, wait,"* she said. "EIN: You mean Employer ID Number, right?"

"Yes," Nicole said.

"Can you please print out the links to the sites she visited?"

"Yes. But it could be a little while; there's a lot of information."

"Just print some of the EIN data for now," Luna specified. Nicole nodded and began processing the request.

"So you think Wu was going to send you something about Bekka's financial background?" Tiago asked Luna.

"Maybe," Luna replied. "I wondered how Bekka's museum got close to such an upscale part of Downtown. She said she got loans for it."

"Now it's a question of *how* she got the loans," Tiago said.

Luna nodded. "And I think I have a pretty good idea," she replied.

CHAPTER TWENTY-THREE

Counting On It

On Monday, the medical examiner determined that Quinn Wu died the same way as Hector Luz: From blunt-force trauma. Wu's funeral was set for a few days later. And Luna tried to remain as low-key as possible (which meant staying away from the museum). But she was more determined than ever to stop Kelvin Frost, and continued to pour herself into more research.

Luna remembered Shandon Sayers, the original beneficiary of the $50,000 payout. Sayers had cancer, which made Luna wonder if it was a pre-existing condition, who was her doctor, and who her life insurance beneficiaries were (assuming she was insured). Luna made several phone calls to Mobile, Alabama to find out more about Sayers.

The day of Quinn Wu's funeral, Luna took a cab to the cemetery. She waited beneath a weeping willow tree that was a good distance from the graveside service. When the burial ended, she remained in place until most of the bereaved left. Then she made her move towards....

"Bekka."

Bekka heard Luna's voice and turned. Dressed appropriately in black, Bekka looked older and more mature than when wearing tie-dye. "Luna," she said. The two women hugged. "How nice of you: To come to Quinn's funeral."

Luna stepped back and removed her sunglasses. "This is bad timing, I know," she apologized.

"Bad timing? I thought you're here to pay your…"

"I have more questions to ask you," Luna confessed.

Bekka shouted, *"At a time like this?!* It's bad enough that the cops questioned me about Quinn's death!"

"I'm sorry, Bekka."

"Why not catch me at the museum, like you used to?"

"I don't quite know how to put this, Bekka, but I think the museum isn't a safe place to discuss certain things," Luna replied.

"Because of the cameras?"

Luna nodded. "I think you might be in trouble, Bekka."

"From whoever killed Quinn, you mean?"

"That's part of it," Luna replied.

"Well, meeting at the museum makes more sense, Luna. I mean, it's safe there. Horus patrols it and has the cameras set-up," Bekka reasoned.

Luna shifted focus. "You told me that you got loans for setting up your business."

"Sure."

"Were they from banks?"

"Yes," Bekka said.

"Did you use your Social Security Number on your application, Bekka?"

Bekka looked confused. After a moment of thought she replied, "I used something called a FINE number."

"You mean an F-E-I-N number? It's also called a Federal Employer Identification Number or an Employer Identification Number."

"I'm not an accountant, Luna. I simply went online and looked for a way to start my business. I-I smoked pot, defaulted on a loan, and ruined my credit history back in the 90's. I knew I couldn't get a loan, with all that hanging over me. So I checked into other ways to get credit; and I found this company that said it was okay to use a FEIN to start a new credit history. I even hired one of its advisors—you remember Sharkie?—as my assistant.

"Sharkie said it was legal and helped me set everything up. She even applied for the loans online; we didn't have to go to the banks. Then I got the loan using the number once. Sharkie got some more FEINs; but she said to use different versions of Bekka with them, like Rebecca, Rebekah, and so on. I got so much that I could afford to setup close to Downtown, where all the big museums are."

Luna realized what was up. She gazed into the clear sky, breathed some of it in, and then looked at Bekka. "That's against the law, Bekka," Luna said softly. "The authorities might look at what you did as an attempt to hide your bad credit. That you misrepresented yourself and used your FEINs to create new credit histories to obtain loans that you otherwise would have been turned down for, had the banks known."

Bekka's hand clamped over her mouth and her eyes widened at the revelation. *"Oh my God!"* she gasped. "I'm going to jail, right?"

"You need to get yourself an attorney, Bekka," was all Luna would say.

Bekka nodded. She wiped away tears that weren't for Quinn Wu, but that were being shed for her own ignorance. "Now I see why you didn't want to tell me this at the museum. It would have ruined me on the spot. The patrons would know I was no good," Bekka said.

Luna moved closer to Bekka and placed a compassionate hand on her shoulder. "I don't think you're "no good," Bekka," Luna told her. "From talking to you for the past week, I think you're a good person. But, you got mixed up with some people who took advantage of you."

Bekka looked up from her tissue at Luna. *"People?"* she asked.

"Sharkie Sayles, for one," Luna answered.

"Just because I have her as one of my life insurance beneficiaries?" Bekka asked.

That disclosure made Sharkie even more of a suspect, in Luna's mind. But instead, she told Bekka, "It's mostly because of the shady financial information she gave you."

"And who else can't I trust?" Bekka asked mockingly.

The next name wasn't easy for Luna to say. "I-I don't know how to tell you this, but Horus..."

"No! Not Horus!" Bekka shouted. Luna let her vent. After a few minutes, Bekka came to her senses. "He gets a lot of that, you know: People thinking he's an extremist or a terrorist, just because he comes from the Middle East. That's why he loses his cool sometimes, Luna."

Luna felt the need to calm Bekka a bit and said, "It's just a hunch. I hope I'm wrong, Bekka. I really do."

"You think one of them killed Quinn," Bekka concluded.

"And the insurance investigator who tried to find out about Kelvin Frost," Luna added.

"Was he your friend?"

"Friend is too strong a word."

"Quinn...was my friend," Bekka's voice trembled. "She didn't deserve to die like that."

"*They* didn't deserve to die like that. But they deserve to rest in peace," Luna said. "And they can't. Not until the person who's using Kelvin Frost to hide behind is stopped."

"You know that I'll help you in any way I can, Luna," Bekka promised.

Luna gave Bekka a hug. "I'm counting on it, Bekka," she said.

"No, *they're* counting on it," Bekka said.

CHAPTER TWENTY-FOUR

Suspects for Supper

The next day, Luna and Tiago strategized over supper. But this time, it wasn't at an exotic, bayside restaurant. And the menu featured a main course of means and motives. It was strictly suspects for supper, served beneath the fluorescent glare of the police cafeteria lights.

"You're amazing, Ms. Nightcrow," Tiago remarked. "Bekka Noon's going to turn over all her records—*everything!* How'd you do it?"

Luna smirked. "Girl talk, detective," she said, through a sip of coffee.

A slight grin curled the corner of Tiago's goatee. He gulped down more of his soda and said, "She knows she's not out of the woods, right?"

"*She knows,*" Luna sighed. "I told her to get an attorney. And I gave her some time to get everything ready, before the local, state, and federal financial departments dig in."

Tiago had his doubts. "But you've met Bekka: I don't think she's capable of this," he said.

Luna agreed. "Her museum assistant, Sharkie Sayles, is probably responsible for the EIN fraud that got the loans. Bekka found her through a shady online credit repair company. I looked into it. Sharkie slipped into the low-key museum job about the time of a Federal Trade Commission investigation of the company 2 years ago."

"Did she get *all* the loans for Bekka illegally? I mean, most people who do business under another name get EINs, but lawfully report the earnings," Tiago said.

"You're supposed to put a valid Social Security number on those loan applications. Bekka said she didn't. She also said that they didn't have to go to the bank to get the loans. From the way it looks, Sharkie looked for people named *Rebecca Noon*—of which there are many—who had good credit; then stole their identities; and applied for online loans. She could have even set-up that phony Miami application, using the character name that she probably heard Bekka blab about all the time."

"God, what a mess!" Tiago replied.

Luna nodded. "We'll know more once Bekka turns over her files," she said. "Bekka also told me that Sharkie's a beneficiary on her life insurance policy."

"Is she on any of the museum's business insurance policies?" Tiago asked. "Sometimes businesses will buy insurance on important personnel."

"I bet Sharkie's on there, too," Luna replied.

"You mentioned that Miami application for Frost. You know, Ms. Nightcrow, Sharkie could actually be K-Fraud," Tiago said. "If so, then what a con: We're looking for a white or Latino male, when it's really a female!"

"Sharkie's definitely K-Fraud in spirit—lying and manipulating, I mean. But in body, I don't think so," Luna said. "Several witnesses, including the beneficiary on the first payout, identified a young, white-looking male that went into the water but didn't come out. And about that first $50,000 payout: Sharkie had to have been involved. I got a call this morning from some of the people I contacted in Mobile. The beneficiary on the claim was Shandon Sayers. She had leukemia. But during remission, she used some of the K-Fraud payout to buy another life insurance policy with an annuity. Then, when the leukemia became terminal..."

"Let me guess: She sold the policy, right?" Tiago cut-in.

"A viatical settlement," Luna told him: "The sale of an insured person's life insurance policy death benefits to a third party with the hope of an immediate cash payment. It's legal, but a hotbed for fraud. Anyway, Sayers became cyber-buddies with Frost through a cancer chatroom. I found out that the cha-troom was sponsored by a viatical company. What's more, Sharkie was an investor in that company! It was also the company that Sayers later went to for her cash-out."

"But if the cancer was terminal, how did Sayers get more insurance?"

"I found out that her doctor lost his license last year for medical malpractice. Maybe he was shady before then and cooked up a report that said the cancer wasn't life-threatening. That way, Sayers's insurer accepted the risk."

"So, Sharkie led someone who called himself "Kelvin Frost" to the chatroom to make friends with Sayers. He made her his beneficiary and then used her to confirm his *drowning*. She got the $50,000, but bought more insurance with it that she even-tually sold—maybe to Sharkie and K-Fraud! They regained the $50,000 and left no beneficiary or pol-icyholder for the cops to question, if the whole deal was revealed," Tiago said.

"*Bingo,*" Luna replied. "I can't prove that Sharkie was originally out to swindle sick people, but it wouldn't be a stretch to imagine."

"Yeah," Tiago said. "She's involved with that credit repair rip-off for sure and knows how to bilk banks out of loans. So, I can see how she takes it one step further and dabbles in insurance fraud."

"And in the end, Quinn Wu wasn't needed to

commit a con because Sharkie had the business and computer skills to do it, too," Luna added. "Quinn had the means but, like you said, no motive. I think Bekka told her about all the easy loans Sharkie got for her a long time ago. But with Bekka being Bekka, Quinn didn't think anything about it. But when I came to town talking about fraud and Hector Luz turned up dead, Quinn put 2 and 2 together, did some financial digging, and called me. Then she ended up dead."

"So Sharkie killed Wu?" Tiago asked.

"Sharkie's the brains; and Horus, the brawn," Luna replied.

"Horus did it?"

"He couldn't take the chance that Bekka didn't blab to Quinn about Sharkie," Luna explained. "Sharkie's the golden goose: If she got Bekka all those loans and collected $50,000 in life insurance, Horus knows she could do the same for his business. Maybe it's been Horus and Sharkie all along. Horus looked up her company online and provided her with a sucker they can both swindle. The museum might be a front for other things."

"If I'm picking up what you're laying down, then Horus killed Hector Luz too, right?" Tiago asked.

Luna nodded. She told Tiago, "I thought about how you picked me up at the airport: You flashed your badge and said you had some new information about the case. Horus used to be a sheriff's deputy and could pull it off, too. But Luz didn't know about

Horus's past or his temper. The poor guy probably didn't know about a lot of things."

"Smart, but not street-smart," Tiago sighed.

"I thought Luz masterminded this!" Luna laughed at her mistake. "I forgot that both of his field cases were solved in small, rural towns."

"Where people are usually more trusting and cooperative," Tiago added.

"Right. So, when some official-looking guy showed up at the airport with a badge and a line similar to the one you told me, Luz's experience told him it was legit—why would a law enforcement officer lie? Horus then either killed Luz in the car or drove him to the townhouse and had the "Hispanic-looking" Frost do it."

"And he could have approached Wu the same way: I mean, drive up to her place; use their mutual friendship with Bekka to get inside; and..." Just then a new thought popped into Tiago's head. "*Wait a minute!* You said Horus was paranoid about being profiled, Ms. Nightcrow. A guy with his Middle Eastern looks—one who hangs around an airport when a big business conference is going on—would probably set off red flags. He'd be picked up by airport security in no time. But Sharkie..."

Luna thought for a moment. "So you think that Sharkie whacked Luz?" she asked.

Tiago snorted, "A lot of security guards I know would be looking at Sharkie as a prospect, not a suspect!"

Luna thought some more, but couldn't dismiss Horus's law enforcement experience. "Still though, detective," she told Tiago, "a badge can have a lot of influence over most people."

Tiago replied, "I don't have to tell you how a beautiful woman can have even more sway."

"Or how a good-looking guy can slow your roll, too," Luna added for good measure.

Tiago grinned. "Getting back to Sharkie, she's not just beautiful, but she's got brains—enough smarts to scam who knows how much in business loans."

Luna continued to develop the Sharkie-as-slayer scenario. "Maybe you're right," she said. "Instead of posing as a sheriff's deputy, she could have pretended to be a reporter or a local insurance representative with information. Maybe it was enough that Sharkie lured Luz to the car that Horus drove."

Tiago changed subjects. "About "the car": We still can't get a picture of the driver or a clear match on the license plate because of the glare and the funky airport camera angle," he told Luna.

"So much for *more cameras* as the answer for stopping crime, huh?" Luna sneered. "Then, we need to check on what kinds of cars Sharkie and Horus own, rented, or..." Luna's train of thought suddenly derailed. Her mouth hung wide open and out came a handful of words: "Darksee Security. Weapons check. *Bingo!*"

Tiago shook his head. "This time, I don't have a clue where you're going."

CHAPTER TWENTY-FIVE

Seeing the Light

Luna's latest line of reasoning led Tiago back upstairs to the Computer Forensics Lab. The insurance investigator took her smartphone from her purse and gave it to Nicole Takamatsu. "If computers can be hacked and turned into basically monitoring devices, smartphones can be too, right?" she asked.

"Of course they can," Nicole replied.

"But the techs didn't find any bugs in your hotel room, on your laptop, or in the rental car," Tiago cut-in.

"But they didn't check my phone," Luna said.

"There are a few easy ways to tell if your cell phone is tapped," Nicole said. "One, the battery loses power quickly, even if you don't use it much or have just charged it. It might mean the hacker is using power to listen to a conversation or to steal information. Two, if the phone doesn't cool off after you use it. The longer you talk, text, or surf, the hotter the phone gets. It will usually cool off when you turn it off. Three, if you hear a buzzing sound during your conversations. And four, if a phone screen just pops on while resting. Notice any of those warning signs, Ms. Nightcrow?"

"I've been so busy the past week that I can't say for sure. I do know that one of Horus Hakim's operatives took my phone and returned it. He said it could be used as a tracking device—which is clearly true because of the camera capabilities alone."

"Could he have put something in the phone?" Tiago asked Nicole.

"Depends on how long he had it. Sometimes, you can insert, activate, and track spyware remotely. This is really true of smartphones. You can send spyware in the form of phony upgrades or apps. So he wouldn't necessarily have to physically mess with it," she said. "My advice, Ms. Nightcrow, is to let us run a scan tomorrow. Even if we don't find anything, we can wipe the handset and just re-install everything new. Or, you can have your carrier do it."

Luna declined. "Thanks though," she said, taking back her smartphone.

Tiago flipped Nicole a thumbs-up for her work, and left the lab with Luna. "Okay, you think your phone is tapped," Tiago said.

"It's probably not," Luna confessed. "But, it's not the tampering part that made me come up with Quinn and Hector's killer."

"What?"

"This will sound crazy, but follow me, detective," Luna said. "We thought it was Horus, right? But we decided it couldn't be because some people would think he was up to no good. But what if one of Horus's other operatives fooled and then killed Hector and Quinn?"

"But which operative?" Tiago asked.

"The one who gave me an airport style pat-down and weapons check the day I visited Darksee Security...*possibly*?"

Tiago's eyes lit-up like a Christmas tree. "I finally see the light!"

"I wish I had sooner," Luna sighed. "Once again, it looks like "the butler did it," as they say. Bekka's and Horus's top assistants used their access and trusted standing to …"

Tiago chuckled, "Ms. Nightcrow, whatever they're paying you ain't enough!"

CHAPTER TWENTY-SIX

Cataclysmic Closing

Another bright blue Miami day faded away and exited through curtains of indigo clouds that fell on the bay. Most tourists headed for bars, the basketball games, or restaurants. So the museums and antique shops in Downtown were closed or closing. The Museum of Modern Metaphysics was no exception.

Sharkie Sayles called in sick; so a Darksee Security operative was dispatched to escort Bekka home. A sedan the color of the darkening sky pulled up. The driver, a white male, put the car in park. He checked his Taser and flashlight. Both were ready to go, if needed. So the operative fired up his iPad for some quick entertainment and waited for his first assignment to begin. It wasn't exactly what he had in mind; but everyone has to start somewhere.

Traffic slowed from its daytime flow to a trickle, with an occasional car or two simply whizzing by. Ten minutes into his watch, the young operative noticed a small white car slow its roll and park up the street from the museum. He thought, *Hey, maybe some action!*

But, as he was trained to do, the operative didn't immediately jump from his car and approach the vehicle. He just watched for unusual activity. There didn't seem to be any movement from within or without the white car.

After 5 minutes of watching and waiting, nothing happened. The operative decided that the car didn't pose any threat and went back to the guaranteed excitement of one of his I-Pad games. When he looked up again, he noticed the lights going off in the museum. Closing time—*finally!*

When the operative saw the front entrance lights go off, he knew it was time to move. Having to drive Bekka home, he decided to first rid the car of any stale air. The power windows descended with an electronic buzz. But, as he prepared to exit the car, the young operative sensed the presence of someone nearby. The sensation came from the passenger side. And so did a fatal flash...*from muffled gunfire.*

Bekka closed and locked the front door. When she turned toward the sidewalk, she bumped into a man in a black polo shirt and matching black cargo pants. But when she looked at his face, her nerves eased off.

"My word, Mr. Kane, you nearly scared me to death!"

"My apologies, Ms. Bekka," Vargas Kane said, in that syrupy-sweet Southern accent.

"*Where's Brett?*" Bekka asked. "Horus said he sent him to pick me up tonight."

"You know how kids can be, Ms. Bekka: The rookie probably stopped to chit-chat with some frat buddies and lost track of time," Vargas Kane answered.

"I hope Horus doesn't fire him for screwing up on his first time out. He's a long way from home, being from Minnesota," Bekka worried.

"It's my fault, for talking Mr. Hakim into giving him his big chance to shine tonight. But let's not worry about all that now, Ms. Bekka. You know how Mr. Hakim wants you out of this area when it gets dark."

Bekka nodded and Vargas Kane escorted her to the white car up the street. He walked over to the passenger side and, in gentlemanly fashion, opened the door for her. As Bekka prepared to get in, Vargas Kane quickly pulled a rag from his pocket and forced it over her nose and mouth. She bucked and clawed, but couldn't break free. After one last muffled yelp, Bekka fell limp. Vargas Kane carefully fit her into the passenger side and closed the door.

After that, Vargas Kane hurried to his trunk, unlocked it, and searched around in the dark space.

Once he found what he was looking for, he slid his arms deep inside and scooped it out. When Vargas Kane appeared, he carried something wrapped in trash bags. He hurried it in the direction of the dark-colored sedan across from the museum. Vargas Kane reached the passenger side and lowered the package onto the grass next to the sidewalk. He quickly tore away the black plastic bags, revealing a slim, blonde corpse.

Carefully, Vargas Kane took the .22 caliber pistol that he shot his fellow operative Brett with and, with a handkerchief, unscrewed the silencer. He put the small pistol into the hand of the dead blonde. Vargas Kane drew the .38 he used on the blonde and ducked into the sedan. He bent Brett's fingers into a firing grip around it. Before exiting the vehicle, Vargas Kane reached with his handkerchiefed hand and took Brett's iPad. Finally, he hurried back up the street to his car.

Vargas Kane was amazed at how easy it all was...*again.* No traffic. And the angle at which the murder and abduction happened was out of view of the one security camera on the outside premises. Perfect planning!

Suddenly, a frightening feeling seized him. When Vargas Kane thought it over, he walked right up to the door to greet Bekka. Maybe a miniature camera above the outside door caught the whole thing! Maybe Horus had more surveillance installed, without telling him!

Terrified by the possibility, Vargas Kane went to his trunk again. He gathered some old rags, a towel, and his emergency gas can. Vargas Kane fished a ski mask from the trunk and covered his face. All set, he headed for the museum. A few feet away, Vargas Kane darted into the shadows. He worked his way around the museum, leaving a trail of gasoline behind.

When he came full circle, the gas can was nearly empty. Quickly, Vargas Kane wet the rags with the remaining gasoline. Then he knotted the towel at one end and soaked it in gasoline too. A single match strike gave him what amounted to an arsenal of bombs. Vargas Kane hurled flaming rag after rag onto the museum grounds. He threw the fiery towel onto the museum roof. And one last match to the ground started a chain reaction that ended with the museum encircled in a ring of rising flames.

Satisfied, the outlaw operative scrambled back to his white car, jumped in, and sped off with his captive, Bekka Noon.

A Familiar Face

It was 7 p.m., but Luna and Tiago were still on the case. Luna sat at Tiago's desk and studied some of the digital photos recovered from one of Quinn Wu's computers. Those of interest included several photos of social gatherings: Pictures of Quinn with Bekka, Horus, and other friends and job associates. Bekka noticed that many Hispanics were also present at the gatherings. Suddenly, Luna thought about Riviera Row land lady Eunice Crossley's original description of Kelvin Frost: He *looked* Hispanic. That gave her an idea.

"If my hunch turns out to be right, you have to get Bekka some *police protection*, detective," Luna warned. "I don't think she can rely on Darksee Security to do the job anymore."

"Right, but let's try and make a stronger case," Tiago suggested. "Without Bekka's files, we've got a lot of circumstantial evidence that the captain may not see as reason enough to assign protection."

Luna and Tiago returned to the Computer Forensics Lab. Nicole Takamatsu pulled up an image from one of the photographs on her computer. "So you want me to do a digital photo alteration of this man?" she asked.

"With every variation that relates to skin tone and hair color, please," Luna specified.

Nicole punched corresponding commands into the keyboard. Luna and Tiago watched with fascination as she isolated the man's face from the surrounding picture. Within minutes, the man's hair and facial features morphed into a variety of new images. "Can we get actual printouts of these?" Luna asked Nicole.

The Deputy Chief Analyst grinned. *"Portrait or wallet-size?"* she asked.

Luna and Tiago left Central Headquarters and headed to Riviera Row. Land lady Eunice Crossley lived onsite, in one of the townhouses. She answered the knock on her door and welcomed Luna and Tiago in.

The investigators passed up the usual pleasantries and got down to business. Luna opened a manila folder that contained the altered photos from the Computer Forensics Lab and asked Crossley if any of them looked like Kelvin Frost. Crossley went through half a dozen with firm "no's." Then one finally got her attention.

"Wait a minute!" Ms. Crossley said. "He looks like Kelvin Frost."

"You're positive?" Tiago asked.

"Darned close," Ms. Crossley answered.

"And you could swear to that?" Luna added.

"Sure. He's got that Cuban or Spanish kind of look: Where he could maybe pass for being white or Hispanic. I bet you that if he dyed his hair blonde or red, he could pass for white. But with dark brunette hair like this, he looks Hispanic—more like Kelvin Frost did."

"Do you remember any other bodily specifics about Frost, besides his face?" Luna asked.

"How *specific* do you want me to be?"

"As much as you can recall, ma'am," Tiago urged.

Ms. Crossley hesitated. Then, with a sheepish grin, she said, "I didn't tell either of you this before because I didn't think it was proper, coming from a woman my age. But that Kelvin Frost...*got me hot and bothered.* You know: Muscles and manners—*lots of manners!*"

"Uh, yes: I understand why you didn't feel comfortable sharing that information, ma'am. But, we're glad you shared it with us now," was Tiago's response.

"Do you mind if I keep this picture of Kelvin?" Ms. Crossley asked. "The face aside, he was a very good tenant."

Luna and Tiago thanked Crossley and left...*without one photograph.* Crossley identified Vargas Kane as the person who looked the most like the Kelvin Frost she rented to. And Luna agreed that if he changed his hair from the blonde buzz cut, he could conceivably pass for a light-skinned Hispanic. She also thought that with some spray-on tan, Vargas Kane could even pass for Swedish or German. He had that sort of international look (which could prove problematic, if Vargas Kane decided to flee Miami).

The car doors shut. The investigators looked at each other. *"Well?"* Tiago asked first.

Luna shook her head. "What makes some people down here so screwy?"

Before the detective could answer, the police radio crackled with an all units bulletin. Tiago responded and fixed the portable siren to the top of his unmarked car. He started up and headed Downtown.

As the car raced along, Luna began to recognize the route. She took out her phone and dialed a number. Luna was confused by the automated disconnected number message she received, and re-dialed.

The car finally entered Downtown, zooming through traffic lights and intersections. After 3 repeated disconnected number messages, Luna stopped calling. As the car turned the next block, Luna could see an orange glow in the distance. It became more distinct as the car moved closer. *"Oh my God!"* she gasped.

Luna realized where the street they were on led to. And why the number she dialed was "disconnected or no longer in service."

CHAPTER TWENTY-EIGHT

More Rubble to Rummage

Bekka Noon's Museum of Modern Metaphysics was a flaming, fiery mess. Rafts of first responders (the police, ambulance, and the fire department) were on the scene. And a crowd of bystanders gathered, but were kept at bay.

At first, Tiago got no closer than the out-stretched palm of the policeman who stopped his car. The detective lowered his window and flashed his badge. The policeman nodded and waved the car through. Tiago parked as close as he could; then both Luna and he hopped out. They ducked under the yellow crime scene tape. Luna followed Tiago to a uniformed officer: An older, burly man named Chuck 'C.B.' Burleson.

"Two fires in less than two weeks. We have to stop meeting like this, "T"," Burleson said.

"You ain't kiddin'!" Tiago replied. "So what's the 411, C.B.?"

"Don't know what the hell to make of the bonfire," Burleson told Tiago. "But on the other hand, it looks like we have a double homicide. Found a car parked across the street. Looks like a john shot a hooker and the hooker shot him, or vice versa."

Something caught Luna's attention. *"A hooker?"* she asked Burleson.

Burleson hesitated to answer, not wanting to release specific information in front of a stranger.

"She's okay," Tiago assured him about Luna. "She's an insurance investigator who's working with me on a case that might be related to this."

Burleson nodded and answered Luna's question. "Like I said, it *looks like* a hooker," he emphasized. "It could be that it was the guy's jilted girlfriend, an ex.., or it could have even been just a robber. What's for sure is that it's another brain-twister for the boys in ballistics and the ME."

Luna asked, "What did the woman look like?"

"Thin and blonde with…"

Luna's eyes widened and her jaw dropped. *"Sharkie!"* she shouted.

Before Burleson could finish the description, Luna rushed to the ambulance. Tiago yelled for her to wait. He caught up just in time, as the techs with the medical examiner's office restrained Luna. Tiago flashed his badge and they backed off. He asked which of the two black bags contained the female victim. The techs pointed it out, and unzipped it.

Tiago flashed his high beam pen light on the exposed portion of the corpse, and Luna looked inside. The blonde's face was grayish and worn; and the hair, frazzled. Some of the shriveled look was brought on by death. But most of it was a result of a hard life on the streets (maybe as a prostitute or druggie). "It's not Sharkie," Luna breathed a sigh of relief, if only because it meant that the prime fraud suspect was still alive.

"Thanks," Tiago told the medical examiner's techs. He turned to Luna. "Look, Ms. Nightcrow..."

Suddenly, Luna saw what she thought might be another familiar face. "Detective, I think I see Horus over there!" she interrupted.

Luna started off, but Tiago grabbed her arm. "Look, don't go running off like that!" he said firmly. Luna looked at him in disbelief. Rarely did Tiago show his tough cop side to her. It was always a shock when he did.

"I thought I had "free run of this town": *Remember, detective?*" Luna scoffed at Tiago's earlier words.

"I know you want to catch these people. But you're an insurance investigator, Luna—a damned good one. You *know* there are rules to follow. Okay?"

It was the second time Tiago forgot to call her "Ms. Nightcrow" during an official capacity. Luna remembered the first time it happened: Over a dinner of

Haitian food that she couldn't pronounce. She allowed herself a brief smile. Tiago saw it, and released Luna's arm. He calmly asked her to point out where Horus was. She did. Tiago saw two other officers huddled around him. He told Luna that they were probably taking a statement, and to wait before they went over.

Luna watched the fire fighters as they slowly brought the blaze under control. The flames began to flicker out, and soon there would be more rubble to rummage through for clues. Luna couldn't help but to wonder whether the search would also be for another dead body—*Bekka's.*

Tiago and Luna finally saw Horus sitting alone next to a police car. Red and white siren lights took turns washing over him; but their security couldn't erase Horus's blues. His teary eyes stared longingly in the direction of what used to be his girlfriend's passion. And for all he knew, it could now be her grave too.

A part of Luna wanted to laugh at how much of Horus's bad boy charm turned out to be bravado. But another part—*her better part*—hoped that if she ever found a man of her own someday, that he would be as worried and heartbroken over her as Horus was over Bekka.

"Mr. Hakim," Luna called. Horus turned toward the familiar voice. "What happened here?"

"I-I sent Brett, one of my young operatives, to drive Bekka home—to ensure her safety. He was always asking me about when I would give him his first assignment. So I called him. Then I talked to Vargie. And look how Brett repaid my kindness: The bastard was talking with a whore, instead of protecting..." A portion of the museum's blackened frame suddenly crumbled into ashes. And Horus buried his head in his hands. When he emerged, it was as a shaken shell of the strapping, self-assured man that Luna sparred with days before. "How did it come to this?" Horus sobbed.

"We have a good idea, Mr. Hakim," Tiago said.
"But we need your help," Luna added.

A Captive Audience?

Bekka Noon felt like she was floating through a groggy, gray sky. Slowly, the cloudiness cleared. And she seemed to descend into cushioned comfort. Bekka felt the familiar fabric of her dress draping her. And her head ached a bit.

From her studies of the afterlife, these were signs that Bekka was alive. If she was a spirit, she wouldn't feel pain or need clothing anymore. However, some of Bekka's other studies concluded that death meant the deceased went to a peaceful, parallel reality.

But when her eyes finally opened and focused, her surroundings told her she was still in Miami... *and in trouble.*

"Ms. Bekka?" a voice called softly.

Bekka was still weak. But she recognized the tone, and muttered, "V-Vargas...*why?*"

Vargas Kane didn't answer. He stretched out his arm toward Bekka. In his hand was a glass of what looked like water. But Bekka hesitated to take it.

"Please, Ms. Bekka," Vargas Kane insisted.

"What's in it, poison?" Bekka muttered cynically.

"Nothing but water—pure *drinking* water," Vargas Kane said. To show her that it was really water, he took a drink.

Bekka took a sip from the glass. Vargas Kane seemed satisfied and set it aside. Bekka still cleared the chloroform cobwebs from her head. She looked around and realized that she was in what appeared to be the cabin of a boat. "Vargas, please: What's going on?" she pleaded.

Vargas Kane stood from the bed on which Bekka lay. "Why did you do it, Ms. Bekka?"

"Do what?"

"Court that...foreigner, Horus!"

Bekka couldn't believe it. "Is that what this is all about, jealousy?" she asked.

"Oh, no: It's about America being taken over... *by outsiders.*"

Bekka threw up her arms. "Then why do you work for Horus?" she asked.

"So I can bring him down!" Vargas Kane growled. Then he melted down into a xenophobic rant. "I learned a lot when I was overseas in the Navy. A lot of them—citizens of the crappy countries we were in— would infiltrate our bases, pretending to want to learn how to clean up their own messes. They would bow and 'yes, sir' and 'yes, ma'am' their way in. Then… *BOOM!* There goes one of our barracks or an embassy. The people we brought in took us out. And now, the people we let into our home are kicking us out!"

"Vargas, Vargas," Bekka groaned.

"With them Latin American leeches bleeding Miami for business contracts, the police are on pins and needles trying to protect everything. They probably think that two explosions in two weeks is a sign of terrorism. And who will they profile? People like Horus! And after a few more explosions, they'll take him down. Then Darksee Security will be mine. All the contracts, all the equipment—*run by an American!*"

"They'll also look into everyone around Horus," Bekka replied. "You, Sharkie, and me: Everything we've said and done will be looked at, too."

"What are the lives of three plain folks like us worth investigating for, Ms. Bekka? We'll be scot-free to do as we please!" Vargas Kane chuckled. "As for "everyone else around Horus": Quinn Wu's dead and that squaw insurance examiner only cares about getting Kelvin Frost's new application rejected.

"Oh yeah, I have to thank you mightily for Frost, Ms. Bekka. Knowing about him was real handy. All them stories you told about trying to write a book on him got me to thinking about how to make some money off it, too. So, when I was back in Mobile, I went online and found somebody to help me setup everything I needed. Got me fake numbers, id, and even a beneficiary to bag me—pardon, I should say Mr. Frost—a big chunk of dough."

"But they said Kelvin Frost drowned."

"Hell, I wasn't even a mile from shore! I went under and just held my breath like they taught me in basic training. Then, a submersible picked me up right on time."

"But why try to use Kelvin again, Vargas?" Bekka asked. "Didn't you know that the insurance company would come after you?"

"It worked before; so, why not try it again in another state and with some new information? I was prepared for the worst though. When the insurance company got wise, I put on my shades, shined-up my operative's badge, and sold that first examiner that I was a sheriff's deputy with a tip about Frost. *And he ate it up, Ms. Bekka!*" Vargas Kane said. "But it won't be long before the cops finally finger the jailbird who lived in that duplex I rented. I found me a white car that looked like his and picked that Mexican examiner up in it. I wanted to pop the other one, too: That smart-mouthed squaw that they sent next. But, it might of stirred up a hornet's nest of suspicion.

"So, best let the cops think that it's terrorists using money from an insurance con to blow stuff up. And the way everything going, who's to blame but a couple of foreigners: The Mexican, for murdering the examiner; and Horus, for scaring the squaw and then burning down your museum because the heat was on from the insurance company. Hell, if everything really breaks right, they might finger Horus for the fix in Mobile *and* for the examiner getting killed! "

Bekka gasped, *"Oh, my God!* My museum is..."

"I declare, Ms. Bekka! That place was a bed of sin, full of ungodly images and idols from hell anyway. It had to be destroyed."

"Just like you had to *destroy* Quinn Wu too, right?"

Vargas Kane just smiled and said, "What had to be done is done."

Bekka gathered herself. She straightened on the bed, and in spirit. "What about Brett? White boy, Minnesota-bred Brett: Was *he a* foreigner too?"

Vargas Kane raised his head toward the ceiling. "I remember a story from the Bible, Ms. Bekka— about Abraham," he said reverently. "The Lord asked him to sacrifice one of his own kin for the greater good."

Bekka shouted, "I don't care! I still love Horus! He's...all I have now."

Vargas Kane tried to reason with Bekka. "With my $50,000 and what can be got from your museum fire, imagine how much we can do to clean-up the country! Why don't you join us, Ms. Bekka?"

"What do you mean *"us"*?" Bekka asked.

"A like-minded group of concerned citizens who

are ready to act—G.O.A.L.: Guardians of America's Longevity. You, out of all of us, have the perfect way out. With your museum gone, everybody will think you're dead."

Bekka laughed. When it let up, she said, "I may be your captive, but I'm not captivated at all. You're washed-up, Vargas. And so am I."

Vargas Kane's passionate appeal for Bekka's allegiance failed. And his blue eyes quickly froze over with coldness. He knew he couldn't count on Bekka not to betray him. *"Washed-up"* you say, Ms. Bekka? Is that how you want it? Well, whatever suits your fancy, ma'am. You'll be washed up then—*on a beach!"* Vargas Kane lethally swore.

"Skipper!" A voice from outside the cabin called.

Vargas Kane slowly backed away from the bed. He watched Bekka like a hawk, as he felt for the door. She remembered his strong arms and hands around her before, and didn't dare move from the bed. Satisfied with her submission, Vargas Kane opened and then closed the door. A *click* confirmed that he locked it.

Bekka Noon was alone in the small, windowless room. When Vargas Kane's footsteps trailed off, she sprang from the bed and began looking for a way out. Then she saw something on the nightstand next to the bed: A small, flat screen. *It was an iPad.*

The dark screen suddenly blinked on. Then it shut off. Bekka watched intently to see what was happening. The screen came on again. And it blinked off. It did this randomly. Is it broken? Bekka wondered. She looked closer at the screen. Between flashes, a message appeared:

LOCATION SERVICES FOR BRETT JOHANSSEN'S iPAD ACTIVATED.

Bekka's eyes widened and she covered her mouth to conceal a squeal of delight at what she thought was happening. It was what she remembered Quinn Wu told her could happen, if her new model I-Pad was lost or stolen.

CHAPTER THIRTY

Troubled Waters

Vargas Kane surfaced from the cabin of what was a 32-foot sportboat—but not *his sportboat.* It belonged to a slim blonde in a black wetsuit. She sat alone in the forward cockpit, with a pair of binoculars glued to her green eyes. She focused on something odd in the early morning mist.

Vargas Kane joined her. "What is it?" he asked.

Sharkie Sayles handed Vargas Kane the binoculars. He focused them himself and saw what looked like a swarm of insects about 50 yards off the bow.

"They look like bugs," Sharkie guessed. But it was an uneducated guess.

Luckily, Vargas Kane knew better. He lowered the binoculars. "Yeah, they're bugs all right. We see them, but they see us...*in hi-definition.*"

The bugs' blue eyes blinked on and off and their "wings" whirred, lifting them up and in a flight pattern that broke towards the pier. They buzzed back toward their hive, which was a large, black van parked in the harbor parking lot. Inside, Horus Hakim nudged the throttle that controlled the swarm's flight. He carefully guided them to a landing on the magnetized roof.

Horus rolled his command chair across the floor to another bank of instruments. He switched to a flat screen monitor and studied the image relayed by the bugs (which were actually miniature drones). Horus magnified the image. He fought to control his temper. *"It's him!"* he seethed at the sight of his once-trusted, now treasonous, top operative Vargas Kane.

Captain Mikhailah Alexander nodded and raised a walkie-talkie to her mouth. "All units, it's a-go. Let's move!" she ordered. "But remember that the suspects may have a hostage onboard."

Luna prepared to move out when Horus touched her arm. He looked into her eyes and said, "If she is alive, *talk softly* to Vargas. If she is dead, stick it to him!"

Luna liked Horus's take on Theodore Roosevelt's line. But she didn't reply, except to kindly pat Horus's hand.

Meanwhile, Tiago and Alexander prepared to head out. They drew their weapons. The detective cracked the backdoor of the van and peeked outside. There was no sign of early morning civilian movement in the immediate vicinity of the harbor. Tiago opened the door and waved Alexander and Luna forward.

Alexander stepped outside first; followed by Luna; and Tiago brought up the rear. The trio stopped short of the harbor entrance.

Luna clutched her smartphone. She busily studied its GPS tracking app. "We really lucked out, with the security guard's stolen iPad," she whispered, as she looked for the theft activation signal to register.

"We don't know if Kane has Bekka hostage though," Tiago said. Suddenly, the smartphone screen broke out with a pulsing red dot. Tiago looked over Luna's shoulder. "Is it a lock?" he wanted to know.

Luna said, "Looks that way."

"Then lead the way," Alexander commanded.

Luna, Alexander, and Tiago entered the harbor and weaved their way through the maze of docked watercraft. Luna stopped, checked the tracking screen, and pointed out the source. It was from a boat. Luna pointed out the location. "A few berths ahead!" she said.

Everyone picked up speed, and hoped to get to the boat before it...

"*Cast off!*" Vargas Kane gave the order.

"Aye, skipper!" Sharkie complied.

Luna, Tiago, and Alexander were too late. From a distance, they saw the sportboat rumble to life and crawl away from the pier. Luna couldn't see anyone in the back of the boat. That gave her an idea. She buttoned-up the smartphone in her back pocket; kicked off her shoes; and stripped away her suit coat. In just her slacks and camisole top, Luna made a break for the pier.

Alexander's jaw dropped. *"No you didn't!"* she gasped.

But Luna did: She stopped, squatted on the deck, and then slipped silently into the water.

"What the hell gave her that idea?" Alexander wondered aloud.

Tiago wasn't surprised. He cracked a grin before he confessed, "My bad, captain: I told her she had "free run of the town.""

"And she took that to mean a *free swim, too?*" Alexander replied. Then she sighed. "God help you, Luna. You're really in troubled waters now."

The sportboat continued to slowly move forward. And that's where Vargas Kane's attention was: Ahead. He watched nervously for any signs of trouble. There didn't seem to be any; so it looked like clear sailing into the Miami River. But the buzz of high-powered motors changed that. Two smaller speedboats converged from port and from starboard. If their dark blue hull bands and flashing red lights didn't give them away, then the disembodied voice that blared through the forward speakers clearly did.

"Ahoy, Ms. Sayles and Mr. Kane: This is The Port Miami Police. You are both wanted for questioning. Heave to and prepare to be boarded!" the voice ordered.

The sportboat seemed to comply; it stopped just short of open water. That gave Luna time to catch up. With increased strokes, she knifed through the thickening water and finally reached the back of the sportboat. With every bit of strength left in her body, Luna grabbed onto the rail and dragged herself onto the swim platform. She crawled into the small passage that led to the middle cockpit and curled into a hiding position.

Meanwhile the police speedboats maneuvered into a flank attack a few yards ahead (hoping to keep the sportboat in the harbor). But Vargas Kane wasn't about to give-up—not with his luck so far. He motioned to Sharkie. She nodded knowingly, and pressed a button on the helm control. A portion of the hardtop cover above the helm retracted. And from within, a small platform holding two canisters rose. Sharkie pushed another button and the canisters zoomed over the bow and into the water.

The canisters bobbed harmlessly for a minute. Then the water bubbled and boiled. Someone aboard one of the police speedboats realized what was going on. Both speedboats began to back away, and a widening lane of escape emerged for Vargas Kane. But instead of taking it, he waited.

"Torpedoes away!" Sharkie confirmed.

The canisters flashed red-hot and screamed toward the speedboat blockade. And about 10 feet away both simultaneously exploded, and a column of water and debris rocketed 40 feet into the air. Sharkie gunned the throttle and the sportboat burst through the damaged police speedboats.

"Praise the Lord!" Vargas Kane shouted for joy. It seemed he'd done it again. That is, until he heard a familiar sound.

CHAPTER THIRTY-ONE

Full Speed Ahead!

Vargas Kane turned around and looked toward the harbor. He saw something rise into the air. And it wasn't just smoke and flames from the torpedo blasts. *It was a police helicopter!* And strapped in the passenger seat was a S.W.A.T sharpshooter. The helicopter cockpit lowered like the head of a charging bull. Then it made a bee line for the sportboat.

"Full speed ahead!" Vargas Kane shouted to Sharkie.

Sharkie complied. And the boat exploded across the river at nearly 60 miles an hour. Despite the boat's pace, the helicopter closed in quickly. The pilot dropped in altitude, hoping to give his passenger a decent shot. But things got dicey.

Sharkie deliberately steered the boat toward a man-made island of high-rise condos. The boat skirted the shore, making it hard for the helicopter to follow without hitting a building. But that game ended when a line of docked yachts blocked a continuous escape route for the sportboat. Sharkie broke back into the mouth of the river. And the police helicopter gladly followed, freed from the canyon of threatening condos.

Hiding in the back of the boat gave Luna time to finally recover. She heard the helicopter buzzing somewhere above. So the boat crew's attention was forward and above, not back. That gave Luna an advantage: The chance of an ambush. But she didn't know how many people she would have to attack. So Luna uncurled from her hiding spot and peeked forward. She only saw Vargas Kane in the bow and a blonde at the helm. Vargas Kane would be a handful, but Luna thought she could probably take the blonde. She ducked back into hiding, and hoped that the helicopter could stop the boat (before she had to risk her life to).

Vargas Kane left the bow and disappeared into the cabin below. Luna sneaked a quick look again and saw the moment she waited for: Only Sharkie was topside. Luna began to come out from her hiding spot when Vargas Kane suddenly returned. Luna dove for cover just in time. She peeked over the wall and saw that Vargas Kane hauled a heavy, high caliber machine gun.

Shit! Luna cussed.

The S.W.A.T. sharpshooter saw Vargas Kane setting up for a firefight. Out-gunned, he raised his rifle first. The sharpshooter adjusted the scope and aimed (with hopes of incapacitating Vargas Kane). Shots rained down, but didn't take down the target. Vargas Kane looked up and smiled sadistically at the helicopter. With an ammo belt in one hand and the high caliber machine gun in the other, he yelled, *"This is how we do it!"* (a line from the popular hip-hop tune), and proceeded to launch a blazing salvo into the sky. Vargas Kane expected return fire and ducked for cover in the forward cockpit. But the helicopter pilot didn't want to risk being hit. The chopper climbed in altitude and temporarily peeled off pursuit.

"Hang on!" Sharkie shouted. Vargas Kane dropped the machine gun and braced himself. The boat suddenly veered starboard and began to circle back. Sharkie performed a perfect 180 degree turn that would force the helicopter pilot to make a wide turn of his own (if he wanted to catch up again).

Luna had to do something to turn the tide. The helicopter would continue the chase. But because of Vargas Kane's tremendous firepower, it would be at a higher altitude, meaning that the S.W.A.T. sharpshooter would be out of firing range.

Luna frantically searched for something to use as a weapon, but found nothing. Suddenly, she noticed what looked like doors on the swim platform. Luna grasped the railing with one hand and swung her body port for a look. She saw what looked like a hatch.

The helicopter finally circled back and continued

its hot pursuit. Vargas Kane regained his balance and his machine gun. He thought he had a better shot, and fired at the helicopter again. The battle gave Luna the cover she needed. She quickly lifted the hatch she found, but didn't need to see what was below. The sound of steady pounding—the high-powered hoofs of nearly 1,000 horsepower propulsion—told her she found the engine compartment. *What luck!* If only she had a grenade or her gun, Luna could blow up the engines and stop the boat dead in the water.

Water! The word sparked Luna's memory. She once drove through a flooded street as a teen. And when the water got under the hood, the electrical systems shorted. Her car stalled before it sputtered to half speed minutes later. *Maybe that principle would work now!*

As Luna edged back toward her hiding place, she saw something: The handle to a small door. A closer look revealed that it was a storage compartment! She turned the handle and opened what was a miniature locker. Inside were only a first aid kit and some rope. But that's all Luna would need.

CHAPTER THIRTY-TWO

Sea Change

Luna grabbed the first aid kit and swung herself back into hiding. She dumped the contents but kept the large, empty metal container. The steady sounds of machine gun fire meant that Vargas Kane's attention was still diverted. So Luna tied the rope around her waist and firmly secured the end to the railing. She balanced herself, and leaned over the swim platform with the empty container.

The churning and spraying water filled the container. And Luna snaked her way back into hiding. She untied the rope around her waist, gathered the container, and inched toward the engine compartment hatch. She opened it and poured the water inside.

Luna waited. Nothing happened. *Dammit!* Now what could she possibly do?

Suddenly, there was a...*BANG!* And smoke seeped up from the hatch. The boat noticeably slowed, but didn't stop. Vargas Kane dropped the machine gun and wheeled around. He saw the smoke and shouted to Sharkie, "They must have hit the engines! I'm going below."

Vargas Kane hurried aft and opened the hatch. He wormed his muscle-bound body through and into the engine compartment. At last, Luna sprang into action. She slammed the engine compartment hatch shut and dashed for Sharkie at the helm.

Luna slammed into the blonde from behind, and drove her into the control panel. The boat veered wildly to port, throwing both women to the deck. Sharkie recovered quickly and scampered from the helm into the bow cockpit. Luna gave chase on her hands and knees.

Sharkie suddenly spun around with an automatic pistol in hand. The boat swerved, as she squeezed off a shot. The bullet missed Luna. And before Sharkie could fire again, she lost her balance and hit the deck. Luna jumped on her, and both women wrestled for the gun. Luna won and wrenched the pistol from Sharkie's grasp. But the blonde grabbed something else: A fistful of brunette hair. She violently swung the owner's head back and forth, trying to break her neck. Luna screamed. She pounded at Sharkie with one hand, while she shoved the other into her pocket.

Luna found her smartphone and hit a switch. A plastic shield burst from the top of the phone. Two pincers popped up, and Luna drove them into Sharkie's hand. The blonde let out a shriek, as 650,000 volts from the phone's Yellow Jacket stun gun case tore through her. Luna then delivered a back kick that connected with Sharkie's face. And the blonde finally went down for the count.

Luna regained enough of her senses to see shore-line racing towards the boat! She dived over Sharkie and back into the helm. Luna had barely enough time to spin the wheel hard to starboard. The force from the sharp turn threw her into the starboard wall. And a wave of water crashed into hull and spilled onboard.

The boat was back in open waters, which gave the helicopter crew the sea change they hopped for. The pilot lowered his altitude. And the S.W.A.T. sharpshooter fired several shots that pierced the hull at key points. Luna came to and crawled into the cabin below for cover. More smoke poured from the boat, until it was dead in the water.

CHAPTER THIRTY-THREE

War of Words

Vargas Kane knew Sharkie was no longer in control topside and gave up trying to fix the engines. After several violent attempts to open the locked hatch, he finally burst through, climbed up, and prepared to get out. But Vargas Kane's forehead bumped into something cold and hard. It was the barrel of a Beretta 70 pistol (the one he gave Sharkie). But the person pointing it at point blank range wasn't blonde or brunette. "Were you hoping that someone else's finger was on the trigger?" Bekka Noon asked.

"No, you're perfect," Vargas Kane said. "You can't shoot. And even if you could, you wouldn't! You got no backbone, Miss Bekka."

Bekka's eyes narrowed and her lips quivered. "Don't be so sure," she warned. "No one could blame me, if I did to you what you did to Quinn."

"Then do it fair and square. Because what I did

to her I did *without* a gun. I did it with my bare hands, Miss Bekka."

Bekka began to shake. The gun in her hands also began to move up and down (which made the chance of an exact shot less likely). It seemed as if he'd done it again: Vargas Kane talked his way into a chance to take control.

But suddenly another voice vied for control. "Don't do it, Bekka!" It was Luna. She slowly surfaced from below deck. "Don't end up like him: A killer who's on the way to jail or the chair."

"Don't *you* be so sure," Vargas Kane countered. "They must use newspapers on the reservation for kindling, instead of enlightening, *squaw*! Because if you read about the way juries see things down here, you'd know good and well that I might just walk!"

Luna wasn't fazed. With smartphone in hand, she carefully approached Bekka (whose back was turned). Luna didn't want to use her stun gun on Bekka. She tried to sway her with words, instead. "Please stay calm, Bekka. You have so much to live for," Luna said.

"*Like what?* Vargas ruined my museum; and Sharkie, my reputation! Even you said that I'm going to jail for scamming the bank!" Bekka cried.

"The cops will like that you're going to cooperate to bring Sharkie and Vargas in. And you still have a man who loves you *for you*, and not because of the things you have. Think of Horus. I saw him at the museum, Bekka. He cried because he thought you were dead."

Bekka seemed untouched. Luna moved to within one step, her finger poised to press the smartphone switch that would unleash 650,000 volts of electricity and bring Bekka to her knees. Instead, Luna dared to reach out with her free hand and tenderly touch Bekka's shoulder. The redhead reacted by relaxing her grip. Finally, her arms fell from firing position. Luna took the gun, and Bekka moved away to tend to the wounds caused by Vargas Kane's words.

As for Vargas Kane, he looked at Luna and laughed. "This isn't over—not by a damn sight!" he promised. "A lot of folks think like me: That this country's being overrun by foreigners."

Luna fired back with a barb, instead of a bullet. "You're right. And a lot of them live on the reservations that *foreigners* put them on, after they overran their land!" she grunted.

"Luna!" It was Bekka.

Luna kept the Beretta 70 targeted and took a quick look over her shoulder. Bekka pointed toward the river. A flotilla of reinforcements sped from the distant harbor. The police speedboats cleared the condo island canyons and finally closed in on the sportboat. It was finally over.

CHAPTER THIRTY-FOUR

Almost Happy

Luna went to the hospital for observation. She was soon released, with mostly bruises and soreness to mend. The next day, she rested and recovered at the Palm Paradise Suites. At about 4:30 p.m., there was a firm knock on Luna's door. She thought she recognized the cadence from before.

Luna raced over and eagerly opened the door to…

…The busboy. "Room service, ma'am," he announced.

Let-down, Luna let out a sigh. "Oh, yeah." She remembered the order she placed an hour ago. Though it wasn't what she *really* wanted or who she hoped to see. At least the busboy left happy (if not from seeing Luna in her short, red satin robe then definitely from her generous tip).

An after dinner cup of hot espresso kept Luna company, as she watched the evening news from her bed. From OKC, to Miami, and even Washington,

D.C., almost everyone was happy with her latest accomplishment: Helping to close the Kelvin Frost case. But Luna noticed the word *almost*: It had a limiting quality.

With $50,000 in the bag for catching Kelvin Frost and 10 percent of the value of the talisman from her last case, something else crossed Luna's mind. It was the words of Lobo (the Oklahoma criminal whose last minute change of heart made Luna a heroine). "What good is being rich, if you can't enjoy it in this life?" Suddenly, Luna knew what she could do to make *everyone* happy.

The next afternoon was cloudy and rainy. Luna sat alone in her car, watching and waiting...*mostly*. Some smooth jazz occupied the rest of her attention. She was no stranger to that; surveillance was part of an insurance fraud investigator's job. It also gave her sore muscles and strained emotions even more time to mend.

When the person she watched and waited for finally appeared, Luna turned off the radio. She exited the car and opened her broad-brimmed umbrella. Not to block the rain, but her face. She walked briskly towards the beat-up old Chevy that the person parked across the street.

The passenger-side window was partially rolled down or stuck in that position. Luna discreetly drew a white envelope from the inner pocket of her windbreaker jacket and slipped it through the open space. It missed the damp seat and fell to the floor, as planned.

The driver of the car was still inside the business he entered and didn't see the drop go down. Luna returned to her car, closed the umbrella, and watched (through rain drops and a few tear drops). It was about 15 minutes before the driver returned to his car. He struggled to unlock it, but finally did and got in. Luna started her car and pulled out.

From her rearview mirror, she could see through the rain streaming down her back window what looked like someone jumping up and down happily—maybe even singing praises in the rain. Luna grinned. Everyone's happy, she said to herself. That is, until she looked in the mirror and saw her lone reflection.

Luna realized that it wasn't long before she was flying back to Oklahoma...*alone.* Back to that cold, lonely loft, only to be off again to investigate some unsolved scam.

Epilogue

It was sunny and 70 something again. Almost the same way it was when Luna arrived in Miami two weeks ago. The long cab ride from The Palm Paradise Suites to Miami International was relaxing. Luna's senses absorbed every last beautiful bit of the buildings and ships along the bay and the palm tree-lined freeway. She arrived at the airport a little before noon and waited to run the gauntlet of security checks before boarding the flight home.

Luna decided to kill time over a gin and tonic and stopped by the airport bar. She saw a few old guys nursing their drinks, as she entered. And Michael Paulo's sexy saxophone version of *Last Tango in Paris* play filled the air.

Luna got the bartender's attention and put in her order. The tables on the main floor were empty and free to choose from. She found a spot near the wide glass windows that provided an up close view of life on an airport tarmac.

Luna watched the planes prepare for take-off.

She even saw one land in the distance. Then Luna felt something land on her shoulder. It was a hand. Luna thought, *Finally, my drink's here!*

Luna looked up, expecting to see the bartender with her gin and tonic. Instead, she saw a dark-skinned man with a trimmed goatee—specifically, the one who slowed her roll the first day she arrived. And he turned her head again, sporting that sexy, white linen suit from their Haitian dinner date.

Luna played it cool though. "Are you here to tell me that things might be heating up?" she asked.

Tiago grinned and took a seat at the table. "I remember someone saying that in some parts of the country, 70 degrees is a heat wave this time of year," the detective playfully replied.

"How did you find me, Tiago?"

"Oh, the same way Santa finds your house and his way down the chimney. Maybe the same way somebody found Jorge De Martine the other day. The same way De Martine found a check for $10,000 in his car. All of it done by watching and waiting, Luna."

"I didn't know Santa gave presents to naughty boys like De Martine."

"He doesn't. But *you* did."

Luna gave a guilty grin and said, "Well, everybody else got something from the K Frost caper, didn't they? Horus got Bekka. Bekka will probably have every publisher hounding her for the rights to tell her ordeal! Burroughs got ratings; Miss Crossley, a picture; my client, a seized sportboat worth more than the $50,000 death benefit he paid out. And last, but not least, The City of Miami Police got the gratitude of the governor and Homeland Security for uncovering and stopping a homegrown terrorist cell, whose founders (Vargas Kane and Sharkie Sayles) may end up *in a cell* for life, if they're lucky."

"But better than all that, I got a vacation!" Tiago proudly announced.

Luna smiled and said, "Congratulations."

Luna's drink arrived. She paid for it and took a sip. "About your vacation," Luna asked Tiago: "Where are you going, the Caribbean—*Haiti?*"

"Been there, done that." Tiago reached into his jacket and pulled out a plane ticket. "I thought I'd take it in OKC."

Luna's stomach flipped and that old tingly feeling started taking her over. "What's there to see in OKC?"

"The second-best team in basketball," Tiago answered.

"*You mean the Miami Heat?* You can stay here for that!"

Tiago chuckled. He reached out and touched Luna's hand tenderly. Like everyone else, she got something from the caper too: The passion she wanted from Tiago. And it continued to grow when he looked into Luna's eyes and said, "You always have your eye on the ball, don't you?"

"That's right. And the balls I want to bounce are yours, baby, day and night," Luna said softly, seductively. She slid her free hand beneath the table to let Tiago know what she meant.

Tiago smiled. "This could qualify as illegal use of hands, Luna," he purred from the petting and patting.

"Tell me, Mr. Referee: What's the penalty for that?"

"You're kicked out of the game."

Luna felt a vibration. But it was from her smartphone. *Damn!* Luna plucked the phone from her pocket...and dunked it into her gin and tonic! "Game over, baby," she said.

"Who are you fooling? *That's a waterproof Sony Xperia!*" Tiago laughed.

Luna smiled mischievously and said, "My phone may be dry, but I'm not."

"Bingo," Tiago replied. He leaned over the table and kissed Luna with all the passion and power that he wanted to—that she wanted him to—but couldn't do before.

"*Wow!* Things are heating up," Luna sighed.

Tiago stopped for a moment. "Enough to fog the lens, do you think?" he asked, looking away. Luna saw what he was looking at: A security camera above the bar. They just laughed; and then, continued to love.

Would it last? Could it last? Luna and Tiago didn't know. But they decided that life's too short not to give love—something neither had truly investigated—a go.

www.ingramcontent.com/pod-product-compliance
Lightning Source LLC
Chambersburg PA
CBHW071408100726
47908CB00004B/1102